MUD, BLOOD, AND BEER

MUD, BLOOD, AND BEER

A COLLECTION OF WESTERN STORIES

L. J. MARTIN

FIVE STAR

A part of Gale, a Cengage Company

GALE
A Cengage Company

LIBRARY OF CONGRESS CATALOGING-IN-PUBLICATION DATA

Names: Martin, Larry Jay, author.
Title: Mud, blood, and beer : a collection of western stories / L.J. Martin.
Description: First edition. | Waterville, Maine : Five Star, a part of Gale, a Cengage Company, [2022] | "Five Star western."
Identifiers: LCCN 2022021875 | ISBN 9781432897871 (hardcover)
Subjects: LCSH: Western stories. | BISAC: FICTION / Short Stories (single author) | FICTION / Westerns | LCGFT: Western fiction. | Short stories.
Classification: LCC PS3563.A72487 M83 2022 | DDC 813/.54—dc23/eng/20220607
LC record available at https://lccn.loc.gov/2022021875

First Edition. First Printing: December 2022
Find us on Facebook—https://www.facebook.com/FiveStarCengage
Visit our website—http://www.gale.cengage.com/fivestar
Contact Five Star Publishing at FiveStar@cengage.com

Printed in Mexico
Print Number: 1   Print Year: 2023

TABLE OF CONTENTS

PART-TIME LAWMAN

It's rather strange, I've never killed a man.

I guess I was an exception as I was nearly three years wearing the blue and being in the middle of many a battle and had never killed a man—and me surrounded by blood, guts, and gun smoke. Although I fired a few rounds I never saw so much as a flinch from them in my sights. So, I guess I should say, "Best I figure, I never killed a man."

I was a mere cook, although they say the army travels on its stomach, so many would say "mere" is a bad description for a company cook. My weapons were normally spoon, iron pots, kettles and chain to hang over an open fire, a gridiron, and lots of sassy replies to those who complained about the day's fare. I am blessed to have hauled a six-foot Shira oven with me when leaving my service, bought surplus for a five-dollar gold piece, and can bake twenty loaves at a time. The oven took up most of the farmer's wagon I'd bought, also surplus, for transportation, but the oven being a hollow affair with its racks removed was well packed with my other goods. Fact is I'm a damn good cook, but you can't make a silk purse out of a sow's ear, or a fine meal out of sour sowbelly, so army cooking was a frustration at the least. A cook can't be better than what he's given to worry over.

How one goes from company cook to town marshal in a town barely large enough to be called such is one of thousands of stories of folks moving west after the war. But I don't imagine many of them involve a fella going from army cook to hash-house proprietor and cook who soon found himself the law, even if only the law in a town of three hundred, all miners other than them who keep them in the day-to-day necessaries.

Those of necessity include our town barber, Josiah Evers, who doubles as dentist and doctor so long as the doctorin' ain't more than a busted wing or leg, and seldom—thank the good Lord—as undertaker. Chester McBean is our hostler and runs the four-stall stable and shoes horses and mules, mostly those from the town's number one employer, the French Gulch mine. Chester is also called upon on occasion to pound out a hinge or buckle or some minor work of the blacksmith. He makes no claim to being an artist with bellows, tong, and hammer but only a get-by if you can't wait to have something shipped in, and "shipped in" is no easy task when two hundred miles from Prescott, Arizona's territorial capital and home to Fort Whipple. I mention Fort Whipple as the passing army patrols are a good part of what keeps the saloon and brothel, and my establishment, afloat. We also have a mercantile and a four-room hotel with a saloon, owned by Howard Hancock, who controls the French Gulch mine—with two cribs out back occupied by a pair of soiled doves. Sally is a trim lass, who's known to advertise with "the closer the bone the sweeter the meat." Juanita is no stranger to *frijoles* and *tortillas,* and if both are not generous with lard, she's not pleased with them—and it shows, as she's at least three of Sally. It's said by those in the know—and I refrain from temptation—she's so laden with wrinkles and crevices that you'd have to roll her in flour to find the wet spot. And that's it, except for a half-dozen humble abodes, all but one constructed of adobe.

The two hundred rocky miles from Prescott is no hill for a stepper, except for the fact the Apache and Yavapai seem to take umbrage at any who wear store-bought boots or wide-brimmed hats to keep the sun off'n their cheeks. And they seem to covet the horses they ride and the firearms they carry.

Not that I blame them, as they've long—generations too many to contemplate—gotten along well in a country damned alien to those of us whose folks came from wet, green Europe. But the spoils go to the victor, and it seems man's nature—at least those who came west from Europe—to keep moving west, even if the country is less than welcoming and hospitable. In fact, this damn country in which I've elected to purchase a hash-house is one where every damn thing wants to sting or stick you . . . or take your hair. So far, I've managed to hang onto mine; of course I seldom venture away from my stove and ten-stool counter, and beyond six tables and twenty-four spindle-backed chairs. Unless someone shouts for the law. Unless there's trouble, and that's where the town marshal badge comes necessary.

Out back, twixt a couple of saguaros as big around as a hog's head barrel and two stories tall, is an eight-foot-square stone building with a door of three-inch-thick plank with a single one-foot-square window therein. I learned the term *hoosegow* when I arrived in Arizona. Like many words we hear the Mexicans rattle off woodpecker-fast, we Anglicize them. Hoosegow comes from cowhands hearing the Mexicans' *juzgado*, or jail. As lariat came from *la reata*. And this stone building is the hoosegow in Bertha's Rest. No need for bars, as the hole in the door is far too small to accommodate a hopeful escaping prisoner, and has little need for glass, as the Arizona weather may cook you but damn seldom will chill you enough for goosebumps, much less separate soul from suet. It's just large enough to pass a bowl of beans and small pail of water through, or the resulting thunder pot back through after the bowel has done its chores. All that said, it's the hubs of hell, and you don't want to occupy it for ten breaths much less ten days. All but one week during my tenure as marshal it's been nothing but overnight drunks and peace disturbers.

The town is Bertha's Rest, and I guess appropriately named as Bertha is buried on what passes for a hill just south of town, along with the rest of her family. Seems she was the only one alive—and barely so and surprising, as you bleed badly when most of your scalp is decoration for some savage's coup stick—when the next party of pilgrims passed. She didn't live long, only long enough to relay her given name to them who soon buried her and put up the grave marker that gave the town its handle. And the real reason it became a town was first a small nearby hot spring that gave weary travelers a soak, and later the discovery of a vein of gold not a half mile from the bubble and pond that became the French Gulch mine.

How'd it happen that old Jack "Jocko" O'Doyle, cook and hash-house proprietor—yours truly—became town marshal? A twist of fate, I'd guess you'd say. Frank Bancroft, our former and first sheriff, got snake bit and soon joined Bertha on the hill. We were without a lawman until three owlhoots from God only knew where decided to fill three chairs in Jocko's, my establishment, and partake of my antelope stew and sourdough bread. I'm proud of my baking, and sourdough is one of my prideful specialties. The three seemed decent customers, although I was wondering their endeavors due to low-slung six-guns and Arkansas toothpicks good for little but slitting throats. Decent until well into the second quart of Buzzard's Roost whiskey. As I am also the distiller, I know the power of my still's drip, so I kept my eye on the three when not flipping cackleberries or pouring the mud that passes for coffee in Jocko's. Watching them closely both because of their soon too-rude behavior and also as they were yet to pay. And they were eyeing my two lady customers. One cannot survive in a burg this small without taking exceptional care of your regulars, and the ladies came every Saturday.

As to ladies, Bertha's Roost is only five strong. Our two working girls, Sally and Juanita, and three housewives. Hortense is our barber's wife and mother of four, a buxom, pleasant lady quick with a smile. Mary Sue Ellen McBean is our hostler's lady, not blessed with children, and rougher than Hortense. She often dresses in a split leather skirt with gantlets to match and a linsey-woolsey blouse sporting more than one patch. She's known to help out in the stable, even to gentle rough stock, and to drive a four-up team of mules with deliveries from mercantile to mine. It's a steep climb and a challenge for many men freighters. That said, she sings to rival a nightingale, and when church is held in the saloon—closed to drinking and whoring on Sunday—she's the main draw due to that angel's voice. Particular since we have no preacher and the rest of us trade off passing along the word best we can. The sermon is often less than inspiring.

It was Mrs. Hortense Evers and Mrs. Mary Sue Ellen McBean who were enjoying lunch when the three owlhoots—who I later learned were Cajun Carl LeBeau, Mac Toynbee, and Black Joe Smizer—walked a little too close to the edge and needed jerking back. I guess he was Black Joe due to his hateful attitude, as he was white as a lizard's belly.

And it was Black Joe's fault I became town marshal.

He shot down another two fingers of my Buzzard's Roost, stood, and crossed the room and, without even bothering to remove his hat, bent low and whispered in Hortense's ear, "It seems you're well equipped to accommodate this here centaur. And this here centaur has a two-dollar gold piece should you care to be in my employ for a short while."

Hortense didn't bother to turn to see who was speaking close enough to singe her hair with his sour breath but rather looked at her lunch partner across the table and asked, "Mary Sue Ellen, what would a centaur be?"

Black Joe didn't give her a chance to answer but did so himself. "Well, lady, he's half man and half horse, and this stallion is hung like a Tennessee stud. Care to earn this two dollars and find out?"

Hortense has always been every bit a lady, so it surprised all in the crowded lunchroom to see she had a stinger . . . she drove her fork into Black Joe's right cheek clean to the hilt.

He stumbled back, his mouth hanging open, the fork springing around like the pole he was using while fishing for carp. It was a good thing it was his right cheek as he reached with his right hand to dislodge the speech impediment, then wipe the blood away, before he reached for his revolver.

It gave me time to cross the room with my weapon, and as I don't cook with a sidearm hanging off my hip, my weapon was a two-foot, ten-pound, hardwood rolling pin.

He only had his hogleg pulled two inches when the heavy rolling pin crushed his hat and dented his skull. He went down like a pint of wet poop from one of Mary Sue Ellen's mules.

This old cook was born in the night, but not last night, and I kept moving, as I know how those who run together think, and sure enough the other two were clambering to their feet.

The one I later learned was Cajun Carl was by far the biggest of the three, so my next target. He, too, was reaching for his weapon and managed to throw his head to the side, and the pin caught him on the collar bone, which snapped like a piece of mesquite kindling. Thus, that gun arm was useless, at least for the moment, until he could try and get his offhand on his weapon.

The third, who I found was Mac Toynbee, was a whisper of a fella, but as Colonel Colt oft times said, his invention made all men equal. The little sheriff's model Mac wore had cleared the holster, but to Mac's surprise and even though I was cocking the pin overhead as if to drive a railroad spike, I kicked Toynbee hard enough to bounce off the wall behind and do a fair job of assuring the world his tainted blood line would not continue. Mac's wide-brimmed hat went flying. On the rebound I brought the pin across the owlhoot's head, and damned if I didn't rend a split over two inches long.

Knowing Black Joe was likely recovering I spun back to see that my favorite whip, mule skinner Mary Sue Ellen, had literally taken things into her own hands and had snatched up a heavy pitcher of water off my counter and with both hands, smashed it across Black Joe's head as he tried to rise. The white porcelain pitcher exploded into a thousand shards, and she looked at me sheepishly.

"Sorry, Jocko."

"Sorry?" I replied. "Lunch today is on the house, and tell your husbands the next meal is on Jocko."

All three hooligans were out of business, and after our barber-dentist-doctor-undertaker used two foot of catgut stitching them up, we deposited them in the hoosegow.

That night the city council, made up of Hancock, Evers, and McBean, invited me to become city marshal, with a caveat it was part time, so part-time pay. Now Jocko's got me by just fine so long as I was willing to occupy a cot in my six- by nine-foot storeroom and eat what the customers didn't, or wouldn't, so the twenty-dollar gold piece on the first of each month, plus rewards all mine should I capture any with posters out on them, seemed a bit of a godsend. Now if I could earn it without becoming a neighbor of Bertha of Bertha's Rest fame, and of our former snake-bit sheriff, I'd be happy. Fact is, it is most times payment just for wandering into Hancock's Saloon after I close up, just to make sure they had no trouble, and they had a one-legged ex-Union soldier setting shotgun so trouble was unlikely, and, the fact is, I would have headed there nonetheless, badge or no badge.

And I was glad for the boy in blue trousers—he still wore his—at the end of the bar with the coach gun in hand as I always was better with a rolling pin than a six-gun. There's something about a scattergun loaded with cut up dimes that encourages peace.

It was nearly a month after the three hightailed it out of town, after two days in the hellish-hot hoosegow, when I learned Cajun Joe had a five-hundred-dollar poster from New Orleans and his partners had three hundred each on their heads. Seems New Orleans was not fond of fellas who helped themselves to the bank's deposits.

Dang if I didn't send eleven hundred dollars flying away down the trail to old Mexico, and them with plenty of time to get there, or I'd be tempted to take my rolling pin and go on the prod.

Even though I hit them hard enough to send them to dine and dance with Satan, they all recovered. So, I still have not killed a man, and, to be truthful, I have no shame saying so.

I guess I am a better cook than a lawman.

BROTHERS, UNDER THE SKIN

July 16, 1860
South Fork of the Yuba River
Negro Bar, California
Jake McKenna stood in quiet consternation, hands folded behind his back, studying the still, moonlit night.

Nary a whisper nor a rustle.

Nothing portends trouble more than silence, and in the mountains, the hush of the wee creatures is a warning, an overpowering roar, to the prudent.

But he shook it off, not wanting—refusing—to trust his intuition, to heed the silence, for he had been pounding the tough trails of the Sierras for three days, and it was rest, not worry, he needed this night. Exhaustion, he knew from long experience, most often brought unfounded energy-wasting wariness that had little to do with any real threat.

This cautious twitch is the little people funnin' me, teasing me for workin' me'sef like one of those bloody mules. Ye be a fool, Jake McKenna. Even in this far-away place, the leprechauns fret a body. He laughed aloud at himself for his suspicious nature.

Like the mules, he too felt hard wintered and humped in the loin, galled to the red meat, sore mouthed, and tender footed. He'd been lathered up and dust dried in layers, so crusted even a frog-filled green-water bath would be welcome. Instead, he stretched and worked the kinks out of his shoulders, deciding to go back to his nightly ritual. He began by kneeling by the little

15

creek and scrubbing the grit from hands and face. The rest of him would have to wait for a deep pool and some quiet time.

Jake had camped near this spot before. Two hundred yards up a clear, trickling creek overlooking the south fork of the Yuba River. Hating to camp on the main river downstream from the filth of the miners who normally perched privies near the river, or more likely who used the river herself, Jake always sought a spot well above on a small clean side-creek.

And Negro Bar was just upstream from where he'd turned uphill. The bar now teemed with Chinese; a people Jake knew little about, only that they did their work and kept out of his way.

Then the breeze freshened, and he smiled as if his own laughter had willed it. *A crisp breeze 'tis the high lonely's answer to a mother's own caress.*

The night creatures took note of the stirring and reassured him further by returning to their serenading while Jake smoothed out his bedroll and kicked off his boots. He surveyed the holes in his socks with another fleeting thought of his mother and the quick tit and tat of her darning needles, then, as he had a thousand times before, put Ireland out of his mind and wiggled his way into a comfortable spot. As if to concede to his slackening caution, a chorus of coyotes yipped in the distance, and, nearby, a white-footed mouse whistled a shrill cry that would have chilled a man who did not know its tiny source— but a sound it would not risk if something was awry.

Jake's blanket lay aside, outside the canvas cover, unnecessary even though the stifling heat had given way to the bracing cool that usually graced the Sierra nights even in the hottest summer. And the refreshing breeze wafted the odor of pine pitch and bough.

And nothing is more reassuring than mind-occupying ritual. As was his habit, he lay back with a small broken pine branch

16

and worked it around the recesses of his teeth—he prized his teeth and wanted to keep them—and as he did so, retraced the events of the day in his mind. He had finished breakfast at the Tennessee House before dawn broke. A treat—a hotel meal—he seldom allowed himself. At two dollars a day wages, twenty-five cents for bacon, beans, coffee, and flapjacks whacked a major dent in the day's income; but the Tennessee featured real cane syrup hauled all the way from Savannah, Georgia, and that couldn't be passed by.

The meal had stuck to his ribs and fueled him as he pushed the mules hard most of the day, crossing the ridge high above the river and stopping at the settlements of Dobbins and Thatcher as he made his way down to the Yuba, then at Foster's Bar when he reached the deep canyon bottom. Then he reversed his direction and led his procession of five burdened animals back towards Marysville following the river downstream until he reached the South Fork, then turned up it. He had learned long ago that if you work an animal hard, he keeps his mind on his trouble and doesn't act up—and he knew he had, many times, proved to be little smarter.

Idle hands are the devil's tools, his mother used to say.

By the time he turned back up the South Fork, the original load he had left Marysville with was down to half, and by the time he would leave Burdeye on its banks, just a few miles on up the tumbling river below him, he would be down to just the mule's tack and his personal items, and the going home—at least home for the mules—would be downhill and easy for him and the animals.

Dinner had been jerky and hardtack, but it was enough with the breakfast he'd treated himself to.

He had hoped to camp in Burdeye tonight, with its single wall-tent saloon, and maybe splurge on a shot of Black Widow or Who Hit John—maybe even a few—but that was not to be.

As it was, he had made what he figured was twenty-five miles today. A hell of a good day considering he'd bypassed two of the toll roads, saving a dollar and twenty cents at a dime per animal each toll, and had to stop for deliveries.

This was the fifth trip he had made for that hard-headed Dutchman, old man Van Dyke, and his Marysville General Store, making deliveries on the Yuba watershed. Gallon kegs of Saleratus—baking soda—and demijohns of whiskey—gallon bottles encased in wicker—were his mainstays on this trip. But he also carried every conceivable notion ordered by the miners and tent stores along the route. Old man Van Dyke still preferred mules to freight wagons when he could use them, for mule trains could avoid the toll roads.

One more trip and Jake would have another stake and could try his hand at the goldfields again.

Jake's thoughts were interrupted by a reoccurring silence, more chilling, in its way, than the banshee wail of the little white-footed mouse.

Then, coming and going through the pines . . . a distant sound, a sound not of the Sierras—a foreign sound carrying sporadically on the wafting night wind. He paused, thought for a moment he was imagining things as he heard the haunting hoot of a long-eared owl in the distance, then the teasing echo came again.

Voices, far away, but raucous. Men on the move.

Jake sat up in his bedroll. Something had been niggling at him since he arrived at this quiet spot, and he was a man who normally followed his instincts, having learned long ago to respect them, and many other things he didn't understand. So he sighed deeply and reached for his boots, struggled into them, then rose to check the staked-out mules and then see what was going on in the canyon below.

He hooked up his suspenders, slung his belt around his

waist—its sheathed knife still in its scabbard—and shoved the Navy Colt he always slept with into the wide leather band.

But first, singing a soothing Irish ballad in a low tone for the animals' sake, he checked the five mules to make sure they were still well picketed; satisfied that they hung their heads in sleep he pushed his way along the trickle of the creek until he reached a spot where it fell steeply away to the dark canyon and the south fork of the Yuba.

The voices echoed stronger. He stood a moment, then the glow of firefly torches topped the ridge opposite where he camped. A half mile across the deep cut of the river, a dozen torches appeared, weird dancing dots of light, then two dozen more serpentined along behind. Specks of light bobbed along down a steep mountain trail. Three dozen hand-carried torches probably meant a hundred or more men, Jake reasoned, for not all of them would be carrying light.

Jake felt a churning deep in his gut. Men moving at night with torches brought back bad memories from his past.

It seldom boded well.

But it was none of his business, and they sure as hell weren't hunting a motley mule train and a trail weary skinner who had delivered most of his goods already.

He considered going back to his bedroll and forgetting the whole cussed thing. He had an equally long day ahead of him. Then he sighed, knowing he would only toss and turn and wonder what was up. There would be no rest for the curious, and that trait had always been the bane of him.

He waded the shallow creek, remembering a rock point on the far side that would give a good view up and down the canyon for a mile or more each way. Sandpaper oaks grasped at him in the darkness, and a few digger pines brushed him as he pushed through, then the outline of the point loomed out of the half moon-lit night, and he carefully worked his way out and sat, legs dangling over the edge.

It was as good as the orchestra seats at the Holloway Theater in Sacramento, if only it were lit with a double row of whale oil lanterns as the stage of Holloway's was.

The procession of men moved in a steady stream of flickering firefly specks across the canyon. But now they moved in silence, an even more ominous intrusion into the deep quiet canyon.

No. This didn't bode well.

Then, to Jake's surprise, a gong began to sound. Not a bell, but the deep resonance of a brass gong rolling up out of the chasm. Its sound echoed from deep in the canyon, its repetition becoming a constant throbbing wail—a keening cry.

He returned to where he'd dropped his saddle and, with the whisper of iron on oiled leather, fetched the Henry out of its saddle scabbard.

Ho Chen arose quickly from his mat and slipped sandals on his calloused feet. The gong could mean only one thing—trouble. Where was his cousin, Tso Sing? The young fool was still playing mahjong. The impetuous youth could never seem to set that particular vice aside, and all of the boy's money went to gambling—at least the amount Ho allotted him, for most of the boy's money Ho sent home to China to Tso's parents.

Negro Bar was none of Ho's concern he quickly decided, for he was here only to collect workers for a new canal farther south off the American River. He stepped outside the tent he had been provided by the deferential Chinese miners—most of whom owed him in one way or the other, for Ho was the most successful Chinese labor contractor in California—and searched the darkness for his young cousin Tso. The camp roiled with the bustle of moving celestials, most of whom were gathering their belongings, but a few stood angrily in the center of the dozen tents, shaking fists, picks, pick handles, and shovels at the approaching throng of men.

I hope the young fool has run to the cover of the hillside. Ho then began moving himself. The torches were too close to wait for anyone.

It had happened before to all of them. "Chinese moving day," as the white devils called it. Rout the Chinese; why should they make a living, even if it was from the leavings of earlier miners who had moved on? And it had happened far too often at Negro Bar, not only to the Chinese but to the namesakes and original miners who had all but abandoned the sand strip along the south fork of the Yuba. And relegated to the mining offal of others, still they had to pay the thirty-dollar-a-year foreigner's mining tax.

Ho Chen was far too old and far too wise to be caught up in this white devil revelry, for he had known of too many times when it turned to violence beyond merely running a camp of Chinese off their workings. He searched the dark hillside above with his gaze, trying to remember the lay of the land when they had ridden in earlier in the day. There was a deep ravine, he remembered, one overhung with buck brush interlaced with clematis and wild grapes. There was no time to fetch his mule; the mule would have to take its chances—and he knew the white devils who approached valued a mule far more than a celestial and would be less likely to harm it than him. Hopefully Tso Sing had gone to fetch the mules and was already well out of camp. Then again, probably not. For Tso would have come for him, if he had his wits about him.

In a steady shuffling gait, dressed head to toe in black, his long queue threaded through a black skullcap and bouncing off his back, his sandals slapping at his heels, Ho made his way to the ravine. He entered its deep recess, paused and inhaled the lush green smell of almost solid growth, then began to climb, pausing only to brush spider webs from his face as he did so, just as voices raised. The white devils had reached the camp.

Almost immediately flames arose from torched tents, but not all of the Chinese had run.

Two dozen, picks and shovels in hand, stood their ground. Clubs flashed, picks and shovels swung, and the thump of wood against flesh and bone, iron against iron, echoed up the hill.

This is not wise. Ho watched brave but foolish countrymen fight to defend their camp—then he realized Tso Sing fought among them. *The fool, the young fool. Fool of fools.* Ho moved deeper into and up the ravine as shots began to ring out.

His stomach knotted with fear for his cousin; his fists knotted with anger against the white-devil miners' almost rabid intolerance. Below him, drunken amusement had turned to shrill insane laughter, then to grunts and groans and curses as what the miners considered "fun" became hate-filled intolerance.

As soon as the first shot was fired, Jake broke brush making his way down the steep hillside, following the little creek.

He now knew what was happening and didn't like it. Not that there was much he could do about it. Chinese moving day was a well-worn ritual in the diggings. Every time the miners got a little drunk, and the Chinese were within easy distance, they'd hooraw them mercilessly. It seemed the Chinese ability to profitably re-work the tailings left behind by white miners riled some. And the Chinese had no protection from the law. So far as California was concerned, the Chinese had no legal status at all. A John Chinaman might as well be a side of beef, or a pile of potato peelings, so far as legal rights were concerned.

Jake had no special feeling for the Chinese; still and all, it wasn't right. Jake would get down there, and maybe he could calm them down some.

At least he might be a steady hand among the drunken ones.

Jake McKenna reached the outskirts of the camp as more

gunfire erupted. The miners were outraged that John Chinaman had stood up to them. They drew and began firing indiscriminately. Chinese turned to flee, only to be back shot as they did. Helpless to stop it, Jake, unseen by the others whose attention was riveted ahead, clubbed down two of the nearest miners firing after the fleeing Chinese.

When it quieted, two of the Chinese who had been felled with blows as the fight began regained consciousness. The miners' blood still running hot, they were again fallen upon.

Cries of "Hang the bastards" rang out, chilling Jake deep in his gut. He had seen many an Irish tenant farmer dangling by a stretched neck, eyes bulging, his land returned to the landlord, after the rebellion around Tipperary.

The gunfire had stopped, so when Jake raised his Henry and fired into the air, the shouting suddenly quieted. He climbed on the three-foot-wide stump of a felled live oak, levering in another shell as he did so. The miners had thrown all the cut firewood in the camp into a roaring blaze in its center, and the sandbar was now well lit.

"Y'men are way out of line—," Jake began.

"Who the hell are you?" echoed through the throng of wild-eyed drunks.

"I'm a man called reason, and Mr. Reason says y'ought to just turn these fellows loose and go on back to Condemned Bar, or wherever y'hail from."

"And why should we?" A tall, chisel-featured miner with hair the color of brass and eyes as flat blue-hot as an August-noon sky, stepped out of the crowd. Not only was he a head taller than the others, but his shoulders lay an axe handle wide, and his body looked as if it had been hewed with a double bladed one—his sleeves and pant legs straining with bulging rock-hard appendages.

Jake pointing a stubby finger at the man. " 'Cause what ye'r about to do is dead wrong."

"And you're gonna stan' up against all of us and keep us from doin' it?" the chisel-faced man asked, then spat a gob of chewing tobacco into the sand. "Dead is vat you might be, mick!"

Jake eyed the crowd, many of whom had sidearms trained on him, all of whom glared red-eyed and angry. "Y'll regret it when ye sober up," Jake said, his sense of survival beginning to overcome his sense of outrage.

"Ha!" the tall miner said. "I'm Gunter Rheinholt, made a' pure German steel tempered in the devil's own piss, and I say you bloody Irishmen are little better'n chinks!" He eyed Jake for a moment, making sure he didn't raise the Henry he carried nor reach for the Navy Colt in his belt. Then convinced the man with the Irish brogue was merely flapping his lip, the big Hun turned back to his peers. Some of them glowered at him for they too were Irish—but Gunter Rheinholt had supplied four demijohns of decent whiskey. And the Chinese were the subject of their current wrath.

"Hang the bastards!" the blond giant of a miner yelled.

All ignored Jake, who silently stepped down from the stump. As the miners dragged the two Chinese toward a tall sycamore where others were flinging ropes across a limb, Jake stepped over a fallen miner and made his way out into the darkness.

One of the miners felled in the fight raised his bleeding head but could not rise. "Jake," he mumbled. Sean McKenna had not seen his brother for most of ten years, and it was little more than instinct that told him to cry out to this swaggering man who moved away from him now. "Jake," he called again, but the raised voices of the bloodthirsty crowd drowned him out. In his dizziness, he dropped his face back to the sand.

Jake worked his way quickly up the hillside in the darkness, then turned and rested the Henry against the trunk of a sandpaper oak. The tall Hun, Gunter Rheinholt, directed the hanging, standing apart from the others, his hands on narrow hips, his mouth turned down in a deadly serious scowl. Jake figured the distance at forty yards, sighted on the man's thick thigh, and fired.

The German miner tumbled as if struck by an axe, and the rest of the crowd silenced, backing away, trying to figure the location of the shooter.

"Carry him home when you go!" Jake yelled out of the darkness.

"*Ayee!*" the German screamed with a voice as loud and shrill as the devil's own banshees. Then he collected himself, and his voice rang hard, but shrill, "You vill die for this, you mick son-of-a-whore!" Gunter's voice roared out over the others, then faded to a low moan as the shock wore off and the badly broken thighbone gnawed at him. When he yelled again, pain edged his tone with a quaver. "I know dat voice. You're the bloody bastard who has called himself 'Reason,' and I vill remember you until I shovel pig dung in your ugly Irish face and you vot in hell."

The other men began to yell in anger, and Jake snapped off another quick shot, showering them with sand. Coming from a long line of Irish poachers who'd lived to poach again, he knew better than to fire two shots in a row from the same spot, so he scrambled away. Men dove for cover and returned fire, but most of them had no idea where Jake was on the dark tree- and brush-covered hillside.

Jake moved twenty feet to the side, as a few of the shots had cut brush near his old stand.

Then he called out again. "There are twenty of us up here, hungry for a donnybrook, all with sixteen-shot Henrys. You should be knowin' we don't take kindly to liquored-up fools invading our camp—"

"Your camp?" several of the men called out, surprise in their tone. "There ain't no twenty—" one of the miners started to call out. Then to Jake's surprise another voice rang out off to his left.

"Yes. Twenty," the voice snapped in good, if clipped, English.

Jake stared into the darkness, thankful for his unseen benefactor.

He turned his attention back to the milling uncertain mob. "The Kighthood of Tipperary bought all these claims. Y're surrounded by our guards and trespassing. We could kill y'where you stand, and the law would be thankin' us for it. And we know y'are the devil's own, for y'have insulted the Irish. We may just be shootin' y'down for the slur."

Again Gunter Rheinholt's voice rang out above the others. "Kill the bastards. Do not let dem bluff you, you bunch a' gutless vhelps!"

The camp buzzed with drunken conversation as the miners tried to reconcile what Jake shouted to them against the chastisement of their fallen leader. With the fire taken out of them, they milled in confusion.

But Jake didn't wait; he moved another twenty feet through the underbrush, held his nose to change his voice, and shouted again. "Get the hell off the Knights' claims, or y'll be shot down like dogs."

"Get out," the other voice rang out.

To Jake's relief, the men began to move, releasing and ignoring the two Chinese, who turned and ran, their queues, now only four inches long after being cut by the miners, sticking out straight behind their heads.

Jake began to chuckle quietly. He'd told some bald face lies in his time, but the blarney he'd just spread was the boldest.

Gunter Rheinholt roared out in pain as four of his followers picked him up and began toting him away from Negro Bar. The last words that rang over the sandbar were pained but full of hate. "I vill vind you, Reason, you bloody mick bastard, who effer you are, and you vill vish you vere dead long before you die. I vill vind you," he moaned, then Gunter Rheinholt's voice faded into the night.

Jake stood quiet for a long time as the miners hurried out of the camp.

"And just who, honorable one, are the Knights of Tipperary?"

Jake spun to the side, leveling the Henry at the speaker, who stood only a few feet away.

The man bowed with hands extended, palms out, showing plainly that he was not armed. Jake stepped closer.

"Stay quiet, friend. Let's wait 'till this riffraff wanders on. I don't want 'em to be sneakin' back on us."

With a supposed twenty gunmen hiding in the darkness, the camp had cleared quickly as the miners gathered up the rest of their wounded, including a drunken, unconscious Irishman also from Tipperary. They followed those carrying the ranting Gunter Rheinholt with the broken and bleeding leg.

Jake spoke to the John Chinaman. "You the other nineteen?"

Ho Chen bowed again. "I am Ho Chen. The Gods have smiled upon us this night."

"I would say y'are a master of understatement," Jake said, his face drawn in a tight grin.

Ho studied the tall man with the Henry rifle dangling casually at his side, the man who had been more than willing to use the white devil's tool, and wondered if he was a man to be trusted, or merely a white man who had his own hatchet to grind.

Ho spoke quietly, knowing that, no matter what the man's motivation, he owed him for his bravery this night. "I am missing a cousin. As soon as I find the foolish one, I will share a bottle of warm brandy with you . . . if it survived the fire."

"Obliged," Jake said, willing to share a drink with this rather creative man—in fact, at the moment, willing to share a drink with the devil himself. He followed Ho Chen down the hillside.

A dozen Chinese lay dead or seriously wounded around the burned-out camp. Among them, Ho Chen found his cousin, Tso Sing—and he was not among the lucky who survived. A small entrance wound in his back was overshadowed by the gaping fist-sized chunk blown out of his chest. Ho Chen carefully closed the young man's eyes, then rested his hand on the boy's cheek for a moment.

"I'm sorry about the lad," Jake said, feeling the man's pain, and in that moment, he began to feel for the Chinese . . . all of them. Somehow, the way they had been treated reminded him of how the tenant farmers of his homeland had been looked down upon by their land-owning masters, expected to bow their heads in reverence each time their "betters" passed. It sickened him then, and it sickened him now.

"I have promised you brandy," Ho Chen said and rose from where he kneeled by his dead cousin. "The others will tend to the dead. He is fortunate to be among his honorable ancestors . . . none of whom are white devils." Ho Chen glanced up at the taller Jake. "I am sorry. I have been impolite."

"No apologies needed. I understand. Many among the whites may be . . . just that. That big German would sure as hell qualify in the devil category."

"I know this man Rheinholt, Mr. Reason—"

"The name is McKenna," Jake said, deciding he could trust this odd little man.

"Mr. McKenna, then. I know this man, Rheinholt, and he is, as you whites say, a madman. What God gave him in size, He took away in other ways. He has long been among the worst in the camps. He will ride a hundred miles to hurt the innocent among my people. Heed his warning and watch behind."

"He's a bit under the weather at the moment," Jake said with a low chuckle. "I don't think he'll be stalking anyone."

"Nevertheless, he will heal, and when he does, he will not rest—"

"That'll be my worry, not yers. Besides, my friend, he'll be hunting Mr. Reason . . . and let's just keep him believing that's the man who shot him."

"As you wish, Mr. McKenna . . . brandy?" Ho Chen said, remembering his promise, and turned toward his smoldering tent to filter through its charred remains. He hesitated, turning back to the big Irishman. "You have made a terrible enemy today."

"He, and his kind, were our enemy long before today."

"That is true. I only wish my young cousin had more good sense."

"Courage besot with pride is the curse of all men who want to change things."

"Courage is very expensive, Mr. McKenna."

"It, and pride, always have been, Mr. Ho Chen. Where's that brandy?"

MAYBE DEAD AIN'T SO BAD?

Maybe dead ain't so bad?

How long can a fella hurt before he decides to take his chances on heaven or hell?

Of course, living the life I've chosen, hell would likely be my fate.

I've been wanderin' this cursed desert for more'n a week, if I'm countin' right. Wandering has come after being in my own prospecting camp for more than two weeks, busting rock, looking for white quartz and, when finding it, hoping it's harboring that yellow metal that makes us all a little crazy.

And the last three days since I was forced to leave my dry camp—thanks to a nearby trickle of a spring giving up its trickle—have been without a whisper of water. The bacon is long et, the flour and dried prunes long gone. Last meal I had was the tail of a fat chuckwalla lizard, and it only four bites or so.

I'm beginning to wonder if my thinking has gone wrong with the lack of moisture as seems proven by my choice of direction. I fear I've wandered in a circle for the last few hours. Damned if a while ago I had to conjure if the sun rose in the east or the west. If that ain't thinking gone wrong, what is?

Sonoran sun's been too much to stand, so I've been travelling in the night. Cool is the good of it, not being able to see distant landmarks the bad.

Hell of it is, the damned rattlers like the night. Howsomever

I'm of late hopeful to come on a fat rattler as he'd give me some sustenance and moisture. Should I be able to dodge his fangs, and should I be able to shoot straight enough or chuck a rock to crack his noggin.

Damn head's been hurting, aching, and eyesight is failing; both sure signs of dying of thirst.

Horse gave out on me after four days without water—I had to favor myself over him, and the last days in camp he went dry. Dry year, known water holes gone to dust. Which is why I gave up prospecting and decided to head for civilization. If the trading post in Skull Valley can be called a touch of humanity, and some would say it's anything but. Had I not been so damned fond of Horse—only name he ever had—I woulda used my noggin and my hip knife and cut out his loins to feed me on my trek. Now I think myself a damn fool for not doing so.

I'm dragging feet and wavering so much I'm tempted to discard the small satchel strapped to my back. But, should I survive, it will make living far more tolerable.

I'm running out of juice, I ain't made water in two days, and my stream then was weak and brown as coyote scat, the last wee flow I had. My lips are cracking, and I'm guessing my tongue will soon do the same. And it seems if I had anything to swallow, I couldn't as my throat is closing, or seems so. It's getting hard to focus. I chucked my '66 Winchester some miles back and my Navy Colt seems to weigh more than a body can stand. What the hell good is long-range shooting if your vision is going to hell?

To add injury to insult, I fainted in the night. Guess it was passing out, as I awoke with my face in the sand and had fallen hunkered up to a damned cholla cactus, and my arm and left side are full of thorns or spines or whatever the hell the painful little bastards are called. The cholla has barbs like a fishhook and pulling them is followed by a spurt of blood, and blood is moisture, and I can't afford losing any. But it's a quandary, as I can't stand the pain of them.

It seems I've been laying here bemoaning my fate for many hours, but I've already stumbled along most the night, and night should be nigh ending, and now my eyes are beginning to see light over the slight rise ahead. So, I cuddle into an indentation in the sand, hopefully in the shade of a low rock ledge, thinking this is as good a place as any to have my bones bleach.

Movement?

What is moving there, maybe fifty feet from my makeshift bed?

I manage to free the Colt and, flat on my belly, with both hands steadying it, bring it to bear on the critter. I don't care if it's a chuckwalla lizard or a wild burro—and in my condition I can hardly tell the difference—it's movement; it's alive; I'm trying a shot. I gotta eat and more so get liquid from critter or plant.

The Colt roars and bucks in my hand, and the movement disappears. I can't have missed at this distance, can I? There was a day when I could have nicked your ear, a purpose, at fifty feet.

I manage to get the Colt reseated in its holster, get my knees under me, and, with the help of a boulder, hump up to my feet. Every damn joint in my body is screaming at me, "don't move," but if I don't, I know this may be my last day before Beelzebub funs my sorry soul with some torture.

So, I stumble forward. Hard to walk when you're dragging feet and your path is scattered with rocks and undergrowth, but I manage to cover the distance.

The sun is now making long shadows of the mesquite and saguaro. And I catch a little dawn sun reflection from the sand ahead.

A few steps and I lean down, both hands on my knees.

Damned if that don't look like a spot of blood. Dark, wet, not enough sun for color yet, but what else could it be? I'm tempted to drop to my belly and try and suck up the wetness, but if it's blood there's likely a lot more of it ahead.

So, I straighten back up and stumble forward. It's minutes, more light, and some hard going dodging cholla and ocotillo before I smile wide, even though it cracks my lips to do so.

A javelina. A fat little gift from God, it is nosed into a cholla, unmoving and going cold.

I've never favored the little pigs, and no one I know does, not even the Apache. But when the choice is starve or eat the foul carrion eaters, it's eat away.

Pull my knife from its sheath and begin the task of gutting the tough, twenty-five-pound critter, careful to stay away from his scent glands. He ain't nicknamed "skunk pig" for nothing. I don't drink his blood but do wet my lips. I still have flint and steel and manage to get a fire going, an arduous task in itself, but soon have a chunk of hindquarter roasting.

I do not believe there has ever been a smell more tempting than roasting meat to a starving man. My mouth would water, had I moisture to make spit.

It's beginning to heat up as the sun climbs, and to my surprise I'm only able to eat a few bites before coming nauseous and thinking I'm going to return the pig to the earth by upchucking. But I manage to keep it down. The good news is my headache is going away.

I only have to crawl twenty paces or so to get in the shade of a huge saguaro with nine or ten arms. And I have no trouble falling asleep, with most of a roasted hindquarter cradled in my arms. It gives one some contentment knowing where your next meal is coming from.

Awaking in the heat of the day, I'm wondering if I'm in a Prescott alley and a half-dozen of my soiled dove friends are fighting, screaming like banshees, over my next token. Then my eyes focus and see a half-dozen, but not doves: a half-dozen coyotes in a tangle fighting over the remaining carcass. They are being stoically and patiently observed by a pair of vultures perched on a nearby saguaro.

I'm not high on sharing at the moment so pull the Colt and let one fly in their direction. They scatter like billiard balls from a hard break. I had to think hard on firing a cartridge as I am down to five in the spinner, and now it's four.

I have to reposition myself as the sun is creeping up my legs as shade disappears but do so with a tad more strength. Reaching the shade, I gnaw a few more bites off the hindquarter, and this time it seems to settle just fine. It's hard chewing with little spittle helping. I'm a long way from wet enough inside. I'm still dry as a whore's heart is of true love, and when I push a finger into the flesh of my forearm, the dent stays. I'm stronger but have to find water.

I sleep another few hours, then know I'm having the most pleasant dream ever. Was I dreaming of rolling on a goose down mattress, as blessed as a man can be with warm, soft skin against most every inch of mine, in the Palace Saloon on Whiskey Row in Prescott, with all six of those half-dozen soiled doves? It couldn't be any better.

Then I realize why. A raindrop has hit me on the nose and trickled into my dry mouth, like manna from heaven.

The Sonoran monsoons have been late coming. It's June, and usually the ravines and arroyos are flooded time and time again by now. But this rain, now whacking down on me with drops seeming the size of my thumb, is making up for lost time and desired deluge.

Thank the good Lord. I'm not generally a praying man, but I steeple my fingers and say a quick thank-you. I'm sure it's not my prayers the Lord is answering, but rather those of a much more deserving soul.

It's only moments before puddles are formed, and I'm face down sucking up muddy water, relishing it like it was French Champagne.

I drink so much I upchuck, and with the water some sour javelina gnawings. But water is more important than food, in the short haul. My hindquarter is where I left it, so I have little worry there. Going back to puddles, as rain pelts my back, I suck up more until my deep gut finally settles, and my belly is no longer sunken.

I find a boulder to lean against and, while I rest and recover, think upon my situation. I'm carrying a small satchel, strapped to my back. I haven't been hunting gold because I was in need of the money, I've been prospecting because I had to clear out of Prescott. I've never been the sharpest spine on the cholla, I guess, as my choice of running mates has always found folks a wonderin' about my character. I never did anything a purpose to harm another living soul, if you consider that anytime I did something considered unkind or thoughtless it was demon rum that motivated the act. I guess, however, those being done to don't feel any better for it.

Whiskey, I guess, has not been my friend. Come to think on it, neither has beer or rye or mescal.

And my last thoughtless Who Hit John sixty proof-soaked act was not only thoughtless but damn sure illegal. I followed a couple of hooligans I'd only made the acquaintance of the night before into the Miners and Merchants Bank across from the courthouse and stood watch while they relieved the place of nearly six thousand dollars in paper money. We had drunk the evil brew all night long, and neither my focus nor my thinking was very good, nor had I thunk through the fact that robbing a bank in the light of day with a street full of folks each thinking it was their money flying away was likely not a wise thing to do.

Particularly with the war not long over and every man older than fifteen and younger than sixty being proficient with the firearm, and every man is carrying.

Fool, fool, fool, I manage to think clearly for the first time in a day and a half of swilling as lead is filling the air and not only from the bank, but from half the pedestrians. Thank the good Lord excitement does not enhance one's aim.

And both of my new friends took a couple of pills for their trouble. Lead pills in the shape of .44-caliber bullets, one aimed by a bank teller and one by a deputy sheriff who was on his way for coffee and standing in the door of the Silver Spur saloon next to the bank, damn the lousy luck. Or maybe from some schoolmarm on the street. Who knows?

We light a shuck the hell out of there, and it is only after a mile or so of pounding trail that my new friend, Orval Page, bends face down onto his gelding's neck. I rein up as his mount slows to a walk, spin back, and come alongside him as he tumbles from the saddle. I leap down to help but discover his back bloomed with blood covering his linsey-woolsey shirt, and him no longer drawing breath. As he carried the satchel full of paper money we'd relieved the bank of, I recover it. I say a word to the good Lord to send Orval on his way, then swing back up into the saddle and, with a whoop, give Horse my heels. Mike Shook, my other new friend, has reined up and gives his horse a hooray and his heels as I pound on by.

I note that he, too, is a bloody mess. Only his seems from a thigh wound, and it has colored his trousers all the way to where they're stuffed into boots, and that boot seems full to the rim and splashes out and splatters the ground as he whips the animal to a gallop.

"You got the haul?" he yells weakly as I pass.

"I do! Oscar won't be needin' his share," I yell, over my shoulder.

"Are they behind us?" he yells back, and I presume he means a posse.

I glance back and see no one on the prod. "If they are, they're far back."

We only travel another quarter mile up into the cedars when I again glance back, and Shook is no longer on my trail.

"Damn the flies," I say aloud and spin back to see if he took a wrong turn. In a hundred yards I find him on his face in the trail, his horse gone, along with Shook's heartbeat. He bled out from a lousy wound in the leg. If that ain't a hell of a thing? I'm fresh outta new friends.

So, I find myself with a satchel full of paper money, a hell of a cheap-whiskey hangover, and no destination in mind. I figure it's a good time to get lost in the wilds for a while so, after two days' hard riding, find myself approaching the Skull Valley Trading Post, which is not a stage stop, only horsebacker trails to and from. I carefully study the place and see there's no wire, so, unless someone travels faster than Horse and me, they have no word of a bank robber on the run.

The storekeeper seems happy to see me, although when I offer up paper money, he says he prefers gold. Don't we all, I reply, and he agrees to the bank issue. I buy myself a fine set of saddlebags, a small pan that will double for eating or panning a stream should we find one, a short-handled shovel and pick, a side of bacon, some Arbuckle's coffee and a little grinder, a pot, skillet, salt, flour, some dried prunes, a blanket, and two canteens formerly used by the U.S. army. And I'm soon off to become a prospector, at least long enough for things to cool down in the territory.

That's what led me to be in hell when it forgot to rain, and all the water holes dried up. And me a boy from Virginia who was a damn fool for wandering into a desert knowing not much more than it got hot and there was damn little shade. That, and that damn nigh everything either stings you or sticks you.

So, here I am, long on paper money, short of cartridges, long on hope for the first time in a while, but short on transportation other than my worn boots and shank's mare.

I still have half a haunch but, when I go to inspect the remains of the little pig, find the coyotes and vultures have made short work of him. Sleep was a blessing, but it divested me of additional vittles.

So be it. I've got some strength up, and my head's working enough to know the rising sun means east, and east means back to the Skull Valley Trading Post, where a fella can buy a mount and saddle and head out again.

And the sun is at my back only a diameter over the horizon. It's cooling down to where I could fry an egg on a rock without scorching it brown, so it's time. And the only way there is to put one in front of the other.

I'm praying for altitude, even if it means harder walking, climbing, and am soon out of the greasewood, into some saguaros, and, after an hour, into the cedars. Thank God, now few cacti to dodge.

I don't know if I can stand another run in with spines. My side and arm are burning up as it is.

It's cooling, and now dark, and I'm making fair time.

What the hell . . . As I top a small rise, I spot a glowing fire in a low swale a couple of hundred yards ahead of me. Could be Apache, but it's not like Indians to make a fire easily spotted. I'd guess a white man. That wouldn't normally be a worry 'cept I'm a hunted man. Wanted for the theft of those six thousand dollars in paper money in the satchel strapped to my back.

I'm down to one of my two army canteens full of water. I won't be able to make it through tomorrow without going dry again.

So, I guess I have to put the sneak on the camp and see what's up. Maybe I can steal a horse and then head south; Mexico is looking mighty fine at the moment.

Cedars are easy to slip through. It's a cushion walk compared to cactus land, so I get to fifty paces from the firelight before I get serious and move as if I'm hunting a Virginia black bear. Three steps, wait, listen, then if all's well three more.

Well, it ain't Injuns. Music is wafting my way from the camp. A juice harp if I know my instruments, and I do. My family sat on many a porch playing a squeeze box, a juice harp, and a banjo.

Now, the question is, how many are enjoying the music.

As I near, I go to my hands and knees, and from ten paces out damn if it don't look like a single solitary man, a gray bearded man, twanging and blowing a juice harp. There's an old dog nearby, a good size dog, spotted, some kind of shepherd dog, which must be as old in dog years as the man as he doesn't hear or smell me. And I presume, after days sweating until sweat run out, an Indian could smell me at a quarter mile. The donkey tethered nearby to a scraggly cedar is more alert than either of his travelling mates: he's looking my way, and those big ears are up and tuned my direction.

The donkey lets out a bray that would wake the dead, and the man stops and pays attention to those with superior senses, and I decide it's time to make myself known.

"Howdy the camp!" I yell out.

The old man comes to his feet and shades watery eyes with a bony hand. He yells back, "Hello, pilgrim. Come on in if y'all got your own vittles. This ain't no church supper."

So, I walk to the edge of his fire light. "Howdy. I got me a haunch of pig, but coffee would be a blessing."

He eyes the haunch hanging by my side. Even with that treat in my possession, the hound shows some discretion and gives me a rattling low growl.

"Hush, Albert," the old man says. But he seems doubtful himself. But he gives me a grin with the few teeth he has left. "Dang if you don't look like you just crawled out of the crypt, friend."

"Had me a bit of a bad time. Got caught in that dry spell and had it not been for that monsoon come along my bones would be bleaching. You got coffee?"

"You look like you need more sustenance than just coffee. I got a few hard biscuits should you be willing to share that bone with Albert."

"Your hound is Albert?"

"He is, and the beast of burden is Victoria, but we call her Vicky."

"So, I can share your fire?"

"Put your skinny butt on that rock, and I'll fetch you some biscuits."

I take a couple more generous bites of the haunch and offer it to the hound. Again, his suspicions are reflected in the fact he doesn't leap at the treat but rather slinks back growling as he goes.

The old man digs in a pack and walks over and hands me a half-dozen hardtack chunks and, after I grab another bite, takes the haunch.

"Albert don't always take to strangers," he says and walks over and gets a wag of the tail from the pooch as the pup accepts the bone and moves off into the dark.

"You got no mount?" the old man asks.

"Died on me. I been afoot for days."

"Well, sir, I guess it's a blessing you found me."

"Where would you be heading?" I ask. It's a blessing, at least so far as the hardtack goes.

"Need some supplies, and Skull Valley is a day, maybe day

and a half."

"You mind if I tag along?"

"Wouldn't be neighborly if'n I didn't. What you got in the bag?"

"Just a spare coat and trousers," I lie, as there's nothing there but paper money.

"Good to have spares. Don't see many bright blue satchels."

"That's what attracted me to it," I lie again. First time I saw it was when Oscar pulled it out of a bedroll on the back of his horse and carried it into that bank. He was a positive thinking fella, as it would take a lot of money to fill it, and his optimism was rewarded. The bag was half full.

"I'm gonna saw some logs," the old man says, grabs his bedroll, and starts off into the dark.

"You don't sleep by your fire?" I ask, a little surprised.

"No, sir. Dog and I will find a place, and he'll let me know anyone comes with mischief in mind. It's good to have a friend."

I can only nod at that as it seems I'm yet to be trusted. It's cooling down, as the desert does come night, so I sleep in my clothes, only removing my satchel from my back and setting my revolver and belt aside. I use the satchel for a pillow, so I'll know should the old man get curious and want to take a peek inside.

I sleep the sleep of the dead, with a hound dog—as infirm as he seems to be—to watch over us and with a donkey seeming a better camp guard than dog. And awaken to the odor of coffee boiling and meat frying.

"Dang if that don't smell as good as the Palace Saloon and Café," I say, sitting up.

"You come from Prescott?" he asks, as I stand and stretch.

I'm thinking it wasn't too smart of me to mention Prescott, so I lie again. "No, sir. I never had the pleasure. Had a prospector tell me all about it, and I'm hoping to visit."

"*Humph*," he says, then adds, "I got a chunk of venison frying and coffee done made. You finish off them biscuits?"

"I did."

"I'll throw in a couple more. You got a long walk today if'n you're coming along to the trading post?"

"I am. Where the hell else would I go?"

He doesn't answer but rather forks out a chunk of venison and sets it on a rock near me, then pours a tin cup full of coffee and mumbles, "Only got one cup but I done had mine."

As I'm gnawing the chunk, he asks, "Wasn't you a bit chilled last night?"

"It was a mite cold," I say, giving him a smile and add, "Thanks for this" and wave the chunk of venison at him.

"How come you didn't dig the coat out of that pack to keep the chill off?"

I can sense his suspicion and shrug it off. "Weren't all that cold."

"We gonna make the post we better pick 'em up and lay 'em down."

And so, as he's packed up, we're off.

It's not an easy hike in the heat of day, but it cools some as we head up and over a mountain with cedars and some ponderosa on the high slopes. He shares a bit more hardtack for lunch, and come sundown we can see the lighted windows of the trading post far below.

We camp near a trickle of water that has formed a couple of pools.

The old man unpacks Vicky and is collecting wood when he yells at me, "You know, a fella don't seem to be able to smell his ownself when he gets whiffy."

I have to laugh. "Are you suggesting I use one of them pools?"

He gives me a nod. "They's a chunk of lye soap in that there pack, which I'd share. I've had some beans soakin', and I'll cook us up some supper while you have a scrub."

So, I peel down and wander over and slip in the pool. It's real warm from the day's sun, and in no time I'm all covered with suds. I haven't been quite this happy in some time. Then I glance over after getting the soap out of my eyes, and happiness wanes.

The old man stands with my Colt in hand.

"What?" I say, a little surprised, to say the least.

"You're not a truthful fella, young man," he says, my Colt in one hand, an old converted army model in the other, both generally in my direction. "Last night you shoulda kept that satchel under-head. I had me a peek, and it's full of paper money. And that blue satchel? An old boy wandered by my camp a few hours afore you stumbled in and said some owl-hoots robbed the Prescott Miners and Merchants and filled up a blue sack with paper money. I always favored gold coin myself, but beggars and thieves can't be choosey, I'd guess."

I try a smile, but I'm sure it comes out more a smirk. "How so I'm not truthful, old man?"

"You're a by-God robber, and the hell of it is, I had my stash in that Miners and Merchants as did a lot of other hard-working folks. So, you are gonna carry that poke on down to the post, and we'll wait there for the sheriff."

"Guess you wouldn't consider me sharing that sackfull with you, and you letting me go on my way."

"Young man, I'd rather be dead than cheat all those hard-working folks outta their future. Besides, some of it may be my hard earned, so I'd guess you'd be happy to share my own with me."

I stand up from sitting in the pool. I take a deep breath. "You seem a God-fearing man. I'd guess you'd hesitate taking the life of another?"

"I'd hesitate, but then again, right is right."

"Dang if it ain't," I say with a smile. I'm holding a rock the size of that coffee cup he shared, slightly behind so he can't see.

He's old, and I'd guess slow, and I'm pretty sure I can bean him with the little boulder before he can pull off a shot. He don't even have the single action revolvers cocked.

And, besides, I'd rather be dead than spend the rest of my days in Yuma prison. I'm told it's hell on earth.

I should have chucked that rock underhand, as I try to throw it hard with an overhand but don't even get it cocked much less cut loose when the roar and flash of both of them pistols surprise me.

Next I know, I'm floating on my back.

I manage to get a hand on my naked chest and get a finger in one of the holes there. It's said your eyesight is the first sense to go when you're dying, and I don't even feel the pain, afore all goes dark.

My last thought is, maybe dead ain't so bad. At least I'll be cool and wet.

GLORY BE

For the first time she could remember since she lived with the widow, Glory slipped into a nightgown. The pink flannel nightgown with lace trim and red embroidered roses Cyrus had bought her . . . the only thing he'd ever bought her. She'd never been able to sleep with anything binding her, even if it was considered scandalous to sleep in the raw by all those considered "proper."

And, God knows, there were plenty of those in Cheyenne . . . most hypocrites . . . but proper church-going hypocrites.

But she would need it on, this night, should she wish to be believed, and should folks run into the room after hearing a shot. Besides, sleep was not on her agenda, should the night progress as she feared it would.

She stood in front of the mirror, with some vanity for a moment, reassuring herself. She was trim, with dark Irish-red hair, only the occasional freckle now that she'd reached her twenty-third year, and not unattractive, or so the men seem to think. She needed no corset—her waist natural, and her breasts high and perky, if not overly large. She was not always convinced of her beauty, which men said she had. In fact, she constantly needed to remind herself that others thought her beautiful. The only real flaws in the reflection were neither of her making, nor God's.

Her lip was still swollen and the area below her left eye brownish yellow, rather than the blue-black it had been a week ago, the morning after Cyrus had beaten her so badly after losing his stake at the wheel of chance in the Silver Dollar. The turquoise color of her eyes made it look even worse. Of course, it hadn't been her fault, as she had been in the room reading until she heard him stumbling up the stairs, dead drunk. And knowing he was a mean drunk, she'd feigned being asleep. Maybe that was what made him angry at her, but, the fact was, he didn't need an excuse of late; he hated himself and everyone around him.

Old Eb, Ebenezer Calhoon, had taught her early on, never let a man lay a hand on you, and never stay with or abide one who did, for he would prove many times over to be a man consumed by his own weakness. And Cyrus had proved to be.

Old Eb had been right again.

And she wouldn't abide a weak man, nor suffer a fool.

She slipped the gown back over her head, used it to keep from burning her hand while removing the chimney from the coal-oil lamp next to the bed, set the lamp on the floor, then used its small flame to carefully begin burning the hem of the flannel gown, ever so careful to keep it from flaming up and getting out of hand. When it was burned a foot or so up in the front, she slapped the flame out and made sure there was no life left in any of the blackened remnant. She carefully turned the lamp down until only an eighth of an inch of wick showed, casting a dim glow over the room, then slipped back into the gown and perched herself on the edge of the bed, in the near darkness.

Waiting.

Johnny, the desk clerk, had told her that Cyrus was riproaring drunk again, and she knew that meant he was spending the last of her stake. He'd long ago gone through his.

And it meant she'd have to start again. She had before; she could, and would, again.

46

And if Cyrus added injury to insult again—and she feared, in fact knew, he would—she would be starting again without Cyrus.

Tomorrow would dawn, and the world would take up a new day—without Cyrus.

Beat me once, you're a fool, beat me twice . . . And she would not be considered a fool, nor suffer one. Not ever again. And sure as hell's hot, she wouldn't tolerate any man who struck a woman.

She let herself lie back on the bed, knowing she'd hear Cyrus coming long before he reached the door, and daydreamed of her past, of her ma and pa, dead out on the prairie, their bones now dust, and of old Eb.

Sweet, dear, old Eb.

It's said that men have a sex organ and a brain, but God only gave them enough blood to operate one at a time. But Eb was different. She knew his equipment worked as he was a customer of a couple of the other soiled doves. Fact is, he'd always treated her like a princess . . . like a granddaughter. Except for a year when he went off prospecting up into the high lonely. A week after he left, the widow woman caring for her passed unexpectedly, and she was left to starve. Glory had to take up the life. When Eb returned, no richer than when he left, he was disappointed in her and stayed away for months. Until he finally reconciled that she was a woman alone and had to do what she had to do to keep body and soul together.

Cyrus was wearing his Colt on his hip and had left the little two-shot .41-caliber belly gun on the dresser. She checked the loads for the tenth time, then slipped into bed and tucked the derringer under her pillow.

She'd almost dozed off when she heard him clomping up the stairs and slamming into the wall more than once.

She feigned being asleep, even knowing it would do no good.

She heard him flop into the ladder-back chair, and his boots hit the floor. After a little more shuffling, he grunted and clawed at the covers.

"Glory, you damn whore, wake up."

The covers flew away, and she opened her eyes, rubbing them as if she were just awakening. "Wha—what? Cyrus, that you?" She realized he still had his trousers on, although his collar and collarless shirt were on the floor.

"A course it is, you bloody bitch. Who'd you think? I saw some old fat boy come down the stairs. You working again?"

"No, Cyrus. I told you. I'm a one-man woman now."

"No, you ain't. You're going back to work . . . back on your back." He guffawed drunkenly, thinking himself funny. Then he added, "I believe I'll take on a couple of other whores and be y'all's . . . y'all's manager. I'll keep you in this high style." He glanced around the meager room, then guffawed again. Then he eyed her with derision, " 'Till you get the pox, then you're on your own."

"I've been fortunate so far. I'm still clean. I'm not going back into the life," Glory said quietly.

"My as—my ass. Them bastards stolt all my money—"

"You mean you lost it at the tables."

He glared at her a moment, as if trying to arrange his thoughts, then took a step forward and grabbed her by the throat, dragging her to her feet, raising her up on her tiptoes.

The gun was behind her, under the pillow. No way she could reach it. He shook her. Cyrus was drunk but still ox strong. And that strength was squeezing the life out of her, until he hit her, hard, with a ham-size fist. She slammed down. Her head snapped deep into the pillow. He shook her again, his thick, hard fingers like horseshoes clamped on her throat. She went black.

She awoke with him atop her, having his way, grunting like a hog at the trough. She could taste the blood in her mouth, and her tongue found a deep split in her lower, already-swollen lip. She sucked in a deep breath, and a deeper resolve.

Keeping her eyes closed she managed to snake her right hand under the pillow, sweeping it back and forth as he rutted away, looking for the reassuring cold metal of the derringer. Nothing. Had he found it while she was unconscious? Trying not to be obvious, keeping her eyes tightly shut, she reached with her left hand, and her fingers curled around the cold bone grips.

He collapsed, whispering, "Damn your hide. I can't never even finish . . . you're so damn worthless."

His head was beside hers, his full weight pressing down on her. She wanted to shoot him in the head as if he were a bull; anything less might give him time to break her neck. But she had no choice. Jamming the derringer into his ribs she cocked it and pulled the trigger.

She was shocked when he barely flinched, but then he pushed up, a hand on either side of her, glaring at her.

The room smelled of gunpowder, but the noise of the shot had been reduced by the muzzle being buried deep in his side.

"What the . . . what the damn . . . what the damn hell?" he managed, then tried to raise his right hand to smash her, but it threw him off balance, and he tipped to his right. She shoved hard with her right hand, and he slunk to his right side, then she shoved again, and he went off the bed to his back with a hard thump.

She was able to rise and could make out the red blooming on his side.

"You . . . you shot me. I'm your man, and you shot me."

She swung her legs off the other side of the bed and walked around the foot and stood at his feet, staring down at him.

"You ain't my man, you son of a bitch. You want to hit me again? Get on up and give me another."

"But, Glory, I . . . I'm your man." Then she could see the fear flare in his eyes. She'd never seen him show fear before; of course she'd never seen another full-grown man confront him.

"Get me a doctor," he managed. "Quick, afore I bleed out."

"I'll get one, but I gotta get dressed first. You wouldn't want a saloon full of men to see your woman in her nightgown, now would you."

She moved to a wardrobe and barely got a robe on before the door burst open. She still held the derringer in her left hand.

Sheriff Philby Hogart strode in. "What the hell?"

She dropped the little belly gun to the floor. "He was killing me, sheriff. I had no choice. He tried to burn me to death . . . lit my nightgown afire. I barely got it beat out."

Everyone hated and feared fire. Women passed too close to the open fire bin on their stoves, or the hearth in their cabins, full skirt caught fire, and the burns killed them. Men died from cabin and field fires. Glory hoped to use that fear to her advantage. And she needed it, as whores were disdained and not believed . . . immoral in one way, immoral in all.

"Lies, lies," Cyrus sputtered, then moaned. "I'm shot, Phil. Get the doc, quick."

Hogart walked over and picked up the derringer, broke it open, and saw only one shot fired. Then he walked to the door and instructed one of the men gathering outside. "Go get Doc Ames. Make it quick." Then he turned back. "You only shot him once."

"Yes, sir," Glory said.

His brow furrowed. "How come you didn't use the other barrel, too?"

"He stopped choking me when I shot him."

The sheriff chuckled. "I'll bet he did."

"Them's all . . . all lies. Where the hell's the doc," Cyrus moaned, his voice seeming weaker.

Hogart walked on and sunk to one knee beside Cyrus. "Looks like you're gut shot, Cyrus. You got a chance, but just in case, I'd make my peace with the Lord."

"He ain't never made no peace with me," Cyrus sputtered.

The door filled with another big man, who eyed Cyrus on the floor, then shifted his eyes to Glory. "What did you do, you damn worthless whore?"

Sam Woolems was a hostler and had long been the best and only true friend of Cyrus's. They'd fought in the war together and ridden with the Kansas red legs.

"I don't need your help," Hogart snapped. "Looks like self-defense to me."

"The hell you say. Cyrus tolt me this bitch was likely to kill him. He told me that over a whiskey a couple of hours ago."

"She shot him in self—" Hogart started.

"He was gonna kill me," Glory shouted. "See this eye? That was last week. See this lip? That was tonight. And he choked me unconscious, and when I woke he started to do it again, saying he was gonna choke me into hell, then shoot me deader yet. He put the lamp to my nightgown, said he was sending me to hell where I belong." It was a slight exaggeration, but she sensed things were going badly.

Woolems cut his eyes to the coat rack in the corner, where Cyrus had hung his gun belt.

"Shoot you with what . . . his pecker?" Woolems snapped. "His Colt is hanging over there. Hogart, I didn't vote for your dumb ass, but I'll damn sure campaign against you next election . . . that's only a month away as I recall. You arrest this no-good scum who shot my friend . . . murdered my friend . . . while I get together a jury and get a scaffold built." Then he turned to Glory. "You better make peace with the Lord, woman, not that he'll pay attention to a worthless whore."

Glory could feel the heat climb her backbone, and she glared at him, right in the eye. "I guess you never heard of Mary Magdalene? Then probably not, as the church hasn't been soiled by your presence in a month of Sundays."

"You bitch," Woolems spat and started for her, but Hogart stepped in front of him and put a flat hand on his chest. "Sam, you're a big man, but I'd be a long row of stumps for you to hoe, no matter you got fifty pounds on me."

"Hogart, I'd go through you like corn through a goose," he said but didn't push forward.

Hogart had his gun hand resting on the stag grips of his Colt, a position Woolems took note of.

Hogart's voice rang with authority. "Your opinion, for what it's worth. Now back off." And Woolems did, so the sheriff continued. "Judge Hollingworth will be here in a week," Hogart said. "We'll have an arraignment, and he'll decide if there's to be a trial."

"But . . . but," Glory mumbled.

"No buts, woman," Hogart said. "We're gonna go by the book, and the book says an arraignment, then, should the judge decide, a trial. It'll be fair." He turned and eyed Woolems. "A fair man, a fair arraignment. None of your hooligan friends raising hell about it, understand?"

Woolems gave the sheriff a crooked smile. "I can't do nothing about the rest of the town, Hogart. I'm only the stable hand around here. You're the sheriff."

"And don't you or them other saloon tramps—"

"I ain't no tramp."

"Didn't say you was. Them others. And all of you mind your ways. Miss Glory here will be keeping me and the jail company 'till the judge gets here. Now, get on your way."

Woolems slowly backed out, and Hogart overheard him say to the crowd, "Come on and belly up, boys. I'm good for a round."

"Sheriff," Glory said, a quiver in her voice, "I can't stand being locked up in a little place. My ol' pa used to lock me in the tater cellar and—"

"You can swamp the place out and work around there, earn your room and board, until the judge comes. You gotta sleep there and make it look good, but I won't lock you in a cell, you swear not to run off."

"I swear, I do swear."

"I'll be locking the jailhouse doors from the outside, but if you can stand this room, you can stand that."

"I can. I swear, I won't run." Then she reconsidered. "You mean you'll leave me alone? What if . . . ?"

"Miss Glory, my sainted wife's got a pullet in the fry pan, mashed turnips and taters and gravy, collard greens, biscuits, and an apple pie. It would take a platoon of soldiers to keep me away. You'll be fine locked up in my stout-built jail."

Glory's jaw knotted. "You don't give a hoot if they hang me."

"You'll be fine—"

Doc Ames strode in, his little black bag in hand. He quickly kneeled at the side of the man on the floor, pulled a stethoscope from his bag, and listened to the heart.

"He's got a decent heartbeat. Bullet still hiding out inside. He's not spitting up any blood, but still it might have clipped a lung. Sure as hell it got his liver and intestine. I'll have to cut on him, so let's get him to my office. Maybe a good thing he's unconscious."

"You got your buckboard?" Hogart asked.

"I do. I'll yell down and get some boys to help tote him."

"We're gone, Doc. Some friends of his downstairs, Woolems and a bunch of no-accounts, might be getting a little frisky."

They took the back stairs to avoid going through the saloon.

Sheriff's deputy, Tobias Sweet, was at the sheriff's desk, his feet up, his broad-brimmed hat pulled low over his eyes, when they entered the back door of the sheriff's office and jail and moved between the cells to the front. He had his feet on the floor, looking alert, before his boss entered the front office.

"I heard," Tobias said as soon as they pushed through the inner door.

"What did you hear, Sweet?" the sheriff asked.

"I heard some soiled dove murdered Cyrus Toke . . . shot him. This the dove . . . the lady?"

Glory shook her head in amazement. "Like you don't know me, Sweet. I got at least twenty of your hard earned at a dollar a poke over the last three years . . . you remember that, I'd guess."

"Enough of that," Hogart snapped at Glory. "Sweet's a married man." Then he turned to his deputy. "First, he ain't dead . . . yet. This is the lady shot that worthless gutter mouth, Toke. You got that right, but look at her. You think a little lady like that has a chance against a big lout like Toke? See them marks on her neck? That's from him chokin' the hell out of her. She shot the som'bitch all right, but damn if it don't look to me like he was beggin' for it. What kind of a worthless no good hits a woman like that? Had I seen it, I might'a shot him and saved her the trouble."

"Looks pretty darn bad all right," Sweet said.

"Take note of it. You'll be called to testify. In fact, go find little Willy O'Leary and tell him to bring that sketch pad he's always scribbling on. I want him to draw her and her injuries. Tell him to bring some color . . . red for sure."

"Willy's only thirteen, Phil. He's likely in the hay sawing logs."

"Tell him it's worth a dime to me."

Sweet nodded and headed out.

Hogart turned to Glory. "You have your supper?"

"I had a beer, a chunk of sourdough, and a piece of jerky up in the room."

"Then let's put our backsides . . . pardon me . . . in the chairs and wait for Willy."

"I could use a little something to calm my nerves, should you keep a bottle around."

"That makes two of us," Hogart said with a smile. He reached into his bottom drawer and came up with two tin cups and a little clay jug with a cork in it. He popped it and poured them each three fingers. "The preacher, Noah Smithers, has a still in his barn. Don't slug it back or your tonsils'll burn clean off."

"I'll sip. Thank you."

They sat for a half hour, saying little, until the door opened.

"Didn't know you were in town," Hogart said to the grizzled miner who entered.

"I was out at Juanita's near the river when I heard. Mind if I talk to the lady?" Ebenezer Calhoon was a grizzled old boy with a gray beard to mid-chest and a floppy hat. He was slightly bent, but it didn't keep him from working hard. He was likely the only real friend Glory had since he'd found her hiding out on the prairie, her folks and three other wagon loads of pilgrims massacred by the Snake Indians. He'd brought her to town, and she'd lived with a widow woman until age seventeen, when the widow passed. With no one to care for her, and no other skills, she found herself with rouged cheeks and a low-cut gown working in the Purple Parrot. Until Cyrus swore he was going to take her away from all that.

Eb didn't wait for an answer but walked straight to her, and she stood and gave him a tight hug.

"You doing okay?" he asked and held her at arm's length.

"Good as can be expected," she replied.

Eb turned to the sheriff. "I swung by the Purple Parrot on my way here. Things are getting ugly in there . . . talkin' lynching. That loud mouth Woolems is stirring the coals."

"It'll be a cold day in hell," Hogart said.

"Woolems seems dead set. Some ol' boy come in while I was watching and told them Toke sucked his last breath. That fired them up even more. Woolems had a reata in hand and was taking the thirteen turns while he was yelling what a murdering bitch was this little lady. I got a coach gun and my Winchester out on my mule. You mind if I stand by you, should all that talk bring them down this way?"

"I'd be obliged. You're Cunningham, right?"

"Eb Cunningham. This little filly and I have been friends for a decade."

"Just so you know, she'll have to sit for an arraignment, then a trial, should the judge direct."

"That likely?" Eb asked.

"Arraignment, yes. Trial? Not if I have anything to say about it, and the sheriff usually does."

"I'll fetch my weapons," Eb said and headed for the door.

As he moved to his mule, he saw the crowd forming at the end of the block in front of the Purple Parrot, and it didn't look like it was going to be a prayer meeting. He looked up and down Main Street, wondering if he shouldn't just load Glory on the back and head out. But he knew they wouldn't get far. Not riding double on his old mule. Then, staring down toward the edge of town, he had a thought. He slipped his coach gun from the center of his bedroll behind his saddle, dug out a box of twelve-gauge shells and a box of .44-.40 shells from his saddlebag, pulled his rifle from the scabbard, and hurried back inside.

"They're coming, and I could hear them shoutin' from a block away. Here," he said, and dropped the scattergun on Hogart's desk. "I'm heading out," Eb said and turned and headed to the door.

"Eb!" Glory shouted, shocked at his leaving.

The door slammed, and Hogart moved to bar the door behind the fleeing man, then turned to Glory, who was standing, mouth slightly agape, shocked at Eb's running.

"I thought he was a friend?" Hogart couldn't help but say. Then added, "I shouldn't have sent Sweet away."

"Give me the shotgun," Glory said.

"Not yet. Let's see what they got to say first."

"Then?"

"Then, if it looks bad. Real bad, and only then."

Eb swung up into the saddle, then gigged the mule out ahead of the approaching mob, until he had him in a canter.

Woolems Livery was the last building on the edge of town, and it had corrals on three sides. It was well separated from the closest other building by at least fifty paces. Eb reined up in front before entering and tied his mule to a hitching rail, then moved quickly and dropped the rails on two of the gates fronting Main Street. As he entered the two big swinging doors, he made sure they stayed open. First, he went to the end of the ten-stall barn and opened the back doors and propped them. He headed to the rear of the corrals and opened gates on each. Stock began to wander but seemingly in no hurry.

He picked up the pace and headed back inside. He always carried a flint and steel but of late had been packing a small box of Lucifers . . . much easier than trying to make a flame with the flint.

He made sure they were at hand, then walked out the front. He was more than three blocks from the sheriff's office and couldn't make out the words, but the shouting and clamoring was growing. He waited until he was proof positive the crowd would not be denied, then hurried from stall to stall. When he'd spotted a little mare, he slipped into her stall. She was tame as a puppy and her saddle, blanket, and bridle were on a rack near her stall door. He saddled and bridled her, pleased that she seemed pleased to have it done. He left her and herded the other horses out. Only three other stalls were occupied, and those animals immediately headed out the back at a happy trot.

Then Eb walked to a hay bin and fingernailed a Lucifer until it flamed, then bent and carefully got a flame going in a manger, then another, then another.

He recovered the mare, led her out the front, mounted his mule, put the Winchester across his thighs just in case, and gave the animal his heels. By the time he reached the crowd, they had torn down a thick hitching rail and were gathering on either side to use it as a battering ram. It was a heavy door, but it wouldn't hold for long. He dismounted and tied the mule and mare, then ran to take part in the battering.

Of course, he feigned helping and instead pulled against the other seven men as they tried to align in front of the door. He kept glancing over his shoulder, until he saw flames lick out of the front doors of the livery.

Then, as they pulled the rail back for a second slam into the door, he yelled, "Fire, fire, fire!" It took a moment for the others to realize what was being said, then all stopped and turned.

"Fire!" Eb yelled again.

Woolems was not on the battering ram but was nearby encouraging the others. He turned, his mouth flopped open, his chin hit his chest, then he yelled. "Buckets! Water! Grab buckets. Get the fire wagon. Damn! Everything I own is down there."

Men ran in every direction, except for Eb.

He waited patiently until the crowd were all running toward the conflagration, now with flames licking over the eaves of the second story and beginning to eat into the hay loft.

He strode up to the office door and rapped on it.

"Sheriff Hogart. Eb Cunningham here. That rabble is all down fighting the fire."

He could hear the bar being removed, then the door swung

open. Eb nodded and walked in as Hogart barred the door behind him.

"You doing all right?" he asked Glory, who looked confused but nodded. Then he turned to Hogart. "I'm taking Glory out to my place on Cottonwood Creek. You send a man out to fetch us when the judge is ready."

Hogart didn't look convinced, then walked over and took the bar off the door, opened it, stepped out, and stared down Main Street to see two dozen men running for water troughs and forming bucket lines.

He came back inside and eyed Eb. "You know arson is a crime, Mr. Cunningham?"

"Damned if it ain't. I believe I read that somewheres. Horse thieving, too. You should know I just borrowed this little mare outside. Believe she's one of Woolems's. I was riding out of town heading for home, minding my own business, when I noted that Mr. Woolems's establishment was smoking a little, so I hurried back to let him know."

"Eb," the sheriff said, "Cottonwood Creek is the other direction."

"Dang if it ain't. The good Lord never did give me a sense of direction."

"Pretty damn convenient fire, I'd say."

"Likely convenient for all three of us. That could have got real ugly."

Hogart sighed deeply, then said, "Likely you're right."

"Well, sir, the Lord ain't much on direction, but He works in mysterious ways. You ready to ride, Miss Glory?" Eb asked.

"Don't mind if I do," Glory said. "I ain't exactly dressed for it in my nightgown and robe . . . but I'll make do."

"You'll look fine in my spare trousers." Eb turned to Hogart. "We'll be waiting for you to summon, Sheriff."

"Make sure."

"Yes, sir," Eb said. "It would be against the law to do otherwise."

"*Humph*," Hogart managed, as Eb and Glory headed for their mounts.

DREAMING A WAY

Author's Note: This story is fiction but based on true characters and events . . . events that led to the construction of the Transcontinental Railroad.

Dutch Flat, California
55 miles northeast of Sacramento
August 18, 1860

"By all that's holy, Doc," Theodore Dehone Judah said, pacing the wooden floor of Daniel Strong's drugstore in his excitement, "if what you're telling me is true, there is a way! Damn it, I only wish I had found it." He grinned infectiously. Leaning across the counter, he pounded Doc Strong on the back, then turned to his wife. "I'm sorry, Anna. But this is a momentous occasion."

Anna Judah glanced up from her sketch pad and smiled indulgently at her exuberant husband. She sat in a ladder-back chair, which suited her upright demeanor, surrounded by counters of potions and patent medicines and studied the two men for a moment. She had decided they were much alike. She and Ted had first come across Doc Strong high in the Sierras, where her husband was seeking a route that would accommodate his dream, across the rugged wall of granite—a trans-Sierra railroad. Doc Strong had been on almost the same mission, but his interest lay in a wagon route that would tie Dutch Flat with the gold producing regions of California and the

61

Nevada territories and bring wealth to the community where he was a major land owner. The only road north of Los Angeles that went east crossed farther south, from Hangtown to Carson City, and Hangtown was booming—and very jealous of its place as the only central California road terminus.

They had parted from that first meeting as tentative friends, but more poignantly as soul mates in a quest for a route across the mountains. A way that could make the man who found it very, very wealthy—if he moved with determination yet held his cards close to his vest.

"Then you'll come and take a look?" Doc Strong asked.

"The devil himself couldn't keep me away. Since the day I got your letter, it's been all I could think about."

Anna smiled at her husband's remark. For much longer than that, since they had been in California, it had been all he could think about. A weaker woman would have been jealous of this mistress of Theodore Judah's—a hundred-mile-long railroad through a ten-thousand-foot-high pile of rock. But Anna Judah was not a weak woman, and she was very secure in her relationship and love for her husband, even though half of California called him Crazy Judah for his barrage of letters to the papers and continual preaching about the merits of a trans-Sierra railroad. Even the United States Congress had ignored him on his recent trip there representing the California Railroad Commission and seeking support. She knew better than all of them. Ted Judah was a dedicated man with a fine engineer's mind and had already made twenty-three trips into the Sierra looking for a doorway through the mountains, and Anna had accompanied him on many of them.

Ted Judah would never quit, until the route was found.

Doc reached under the drugstore counter and snatched a bottle of his universal cure, brandy, and brought it up with three snifters. "I think this calls for a toast."

"I don't imbibe," Ted said, "but you go ahead. Anna and I will toast with you in spirit."

So, Doc did. He studied his new friends intently as Judah crossed the room to where Anna sat by the warm potbellied stove, intent on her sketchpad. He had just learned something else about Ted Judah: he was a teetotaler. Doc was glad he had written to Judah, who was California's recognized expert in railroads. Since reading Judah's pamphlet *A Practical Plan for Building the Pacific Railroad,* which the engineer had published with his own money, Ted had wanted to meet the man—and the chance meeting high in the Sierras had been providence. Theodore Judah had graduated from Troy School of Technology and immediately gone to work for the Troy & Schenectady Railroad. He had gone on to become resident engineer for the Erie Canal, then on to build the impossible Niagara Gorge Railroad. Luckily for California, Colonel Charles Lincoln Wilson, who had made his own fortune with a plank toll road and then a toll bridge in San Francisco, had convinced Judah to come West for the building of his Sacramento Valley Railroad, where Judah was still employed as resident engineer. But the job didn't challenge the man, and Wilson had proved to be less of a visionary than Ted Judah had hoped. Wilson was content with a railroad that huffed and puffed its way a short twenty-two miles up and down the relatively flat Sacramento Valley, and his own authority was limited, for he had been reduced from the president to a member of the board of directors when the Sacramento Valley Railroad was almost foreclosed upon by her contractors, Robinson, Seymour & Company of New York. And even now, most of the railroad's earnings went to pay interest on the massive seven hundred thousand dollars in debt it had accumulated and still owed to that firm.

No, Wilson's vision had been blurred by adversity.

Ted Judah won't be employed there long, Doc Strong thought smugly as he sipped the snifter of brandy. *Not after I show him my route. He'll be my new partner.*

"Will you be going with us, Mrs. Judah?" Doc asked from over his brandy snifter.

"Not this time, Doctor Strong. Ted will have to do without me, and you'll have to put up with his camp cooking. I've brought back a hundred sketches of the beautiful mountains, and I must put them to canvas. I believe some new paints I've ordered have arrived at Huntington & Hopkins in Sacramento. I'll wait this one out."

Anna Judah had been on many a trip into the wilderness with her husband. Doc couldn't help but let his eyes drift over her. A trim, well-turned woman, with striking gray-green eyes and a red tint to her dark hair . . . and a true lady, but one who could set a horse as well as any man. He had admired her when he had met them high up on the Yuba River. He was sorry she wasn't coming, for she would make a tough trip a lot more pleasurable.

"Then we leave in the morning?" Ted asked.

"Can Anna get home to Sacramento alone?" Doc asked, then realized it was a silly question.

"Anna could get to the top of the Andes alone," Ted Judah said proudly. "By gosh, if it weren't for my Episcopalian upbringing, I'd have that brandy."

"I'll pour you some tea," Anna said quickly, setting her sketch pad aside and reaching for the teapot atop the potbellied stove. "Then we'll head back to the rooming house, if that's all right with you, Ted."

Ted Judah merely smiled. Anna had a long overdue bath coming and had been talking about it, relishing it, for the last days as they descended on horseback from the high Sierra peaks.

"We'll leave day after tomorrow," Doc said. "That'll give you time to get Anna on her way home and me time to arrange for someone to watch the store. I've got two good mules. Jake Mc-Kenna, the packer who accompanied me on the last trip, is due back in town tomorrow, and I'd like to have him along. He's as good a man in the mountains as I've ever seen, and he's got a fine pack mule to add to the two of mine." He grinned before he added, "And besides, the Irish work cheap."

"Then it's day after tomorrow." Ted and Anna Judah raised their teacups and toasted with Doc Strong.

But Ted Judah stared into the distance, already visualizing the gentle slope that would let him realize his dream.

From the second-story window of the Tremont House on Sacramento's Front Street, Anna Judah could view the river and the Embarcadero. The cold evening air was remarkably clear, and the sun hung low enough it reflected off a gathering cloud cover. The sight was a pleasant distraction as the Steamship *Antelope* unloaded. The seven p.m. ship, early, disembarked its load of passengers from San Francisco. The glorious sunset, peeking through the heavy hedgerow of cottonwoods and oaks on the far side of the river and reflecting off the cloud cover above and the water below, gave the scene a painterly quality that almost took her breath.

And Anna needed a distraction.

Ted had come to an amiable parting of the ways with his employer, Colonel Wilson and the Sacramento Valley Railroad. Now he could put his full-time efforts into raising the money for the survey, but, then again, now raising the money was an *absolute* necessity. They had no income, and the money they had saved would soon run out.

Ted and Doc Strong needed only five hundred dollars to verify the route with more sightings and elevation, but they did not have the money themselves and had not been able to raise even that small amount. State law required that a railroad have subscriptions for one thousand dollars a mile for the mileage to be built—a fifty-five-thousand-dollar commitment to reach Dutch Flat alone—with ten percent of that paid in before they could obtain a charter. That amount seemed eons away.

Anna Judah leaned away from her easel and gave her husband a peck on the cheek, then he headed for the door, pausing only long enough to snatch a hat from the nearby rack and adjust it on his head. "You look marvelous, darling, as usual." Ted turned and winked at her. He was a man given to fine clothes, and the velvet coat he sported was as fine as any available—perhaps in rebellion against his almost destitute youth as a preacher's son. He also wore the latest in gaiter shoes and sported a leather-covered, gold-handled walking stick.

"This time, Ted," Anna said with encouragement. He glanced back and managed a weak smile before he slipped out into the failing light.

Only the night before, at the more prestigious St. George Hotel just down Front Street, he had held one of the innumerable meetings he had called during the past three months—trying anyone who would listen. For the better part of the month before they had been in San Francisco, where Ted had been sure he would easily raise the thirty-five thousand dollars he and Doc Strong figured they needed to survey their trans-Sierra railroad over the mountains. But even though they had met with San Francisco's finest, any of whom could easily have backed the venture single-handed, Ted Judah had come away with only two stockholders, and those for less than twenty dollars each.

It was proving an impossible task. No one seemed interested in risking a nickel to try to cross the great granite mountains with a railroad. The Pony Express was all the talk, as letters reached Sacramento from St. Joseph in only ten to twelve days.

But Anna knew it was more than that.

The shipping interests were against the railroad, particularly the powerful Pacific Mail Steamship and California Steam Navigation Companies, for the lucrative trade around the Horn, across Panama, and up the rivers would be finished. The Pioneer Stage road, a toll route from Virginia City to Hangtown, stood to lose most of its traffic. The Sacramento Valley Railroad and powerful Colonel Wilson were definitely against the trans-Sierra, because they figured Congress should be imploring them to build it, and if Congress would *grant* them the money, then . . . Merchants worried that the flow of cheap goods by railroad from the East would hurt their business. Wells Fargo, Co. would lose horrendously. The Overland Telegraph would not welcome the wire that would be built along a railroad route, and the Overland Stage from Missouri to California saw herself doomed by a railroad. Even the Sitka Ice Company, which brought ice by ship all the way from the Alaska glaciers to San Francisco, Sacramento, and the gold fields, hated the thought of their competitors' product coming from the high Sierra via cheap railroad rates to destroy their lucrative trade. Not to speak of a host of other smaller freight companies who saw doom with the advent of a railroad.

But tonight will be different, Anna assured herself, as she had done so many times before. Sacramento was not so rich as San Francisco—so maybe there were fewer axes to grind here—and the meeting last night had been promising. Collis Huntington, a local hardware merchant, had pulled Ted aside and invited him to drop by his store "sometime" to talk more about his venture. Anna smiled inwardly as she returned to dab on the Sierra scene she painted, for Ted had jumped at the chance and said he would drop by the very next night, tonight.

Again she would spend the evening alone, but better by herself than with a brooding, unhappy man.

Tonight, she reaffirmed. *Tonight he will come home with that old light in his eyes and the smile she loved.* Again, she dabbed paint on the canvas, but the hand she held behind her had fingers crossed tightly.

Ted Judah slipped his watch from his waistcoat and shined its crystal face on the fabric out of habit before he checked the time in the yellow glow of a gas lamp, one of thirty-five recently installed. Six fifty-five p.m., right on time. He had spent the day casually asking questions along the Embarcadero about his host for the evening, Collis Huntington. He had found out little about the man, but what he had learned he liked. Huntington had come from New York in '49, a true forty-niner. Like many, he found himself stranded in Panama awaiting a ship north to San Francisco, but, unlike the thousands of others, Huntington had begun his enterprise there. The six foot-plus, steely-blue-eyed Huntington had walked across the Isthmus more than twenty times, trading jerked beef, potatoes, rice, sugar, and syrup, carrying his goods on his back. He had left Panama with more than four times the money he had arrived with and aboard his own vessel loaded with goods acquired in Colombia. When he finally reached the gold fields, he had mined with shovel and pick for the total of one morning, then returned to Sacramento to get into the hardware business, deciding mining the miners would be far more profitable.

The store across K Street from where Judah stood, just around the corner from the Tremont House, was imposing. Two stories, granite block, with a wide porch opening off the offices on the second floor, a large sign atop the eaves read *Huntington & Hopkins, Hardware.* On the second-floor porch, smaller signs proclaimed Rubber Hose, Belting, Powder, Fuse, Rope, Blocks, Pitch, Tar, etc. And under that, over the entry door and windows, still another sign stated Hardware, Iron, Steel, & Coal.

Huntington & Hopkins was Sacramento's largest hardware dealer.

Ted Judah had been unable to find out much about Huntington's partner, Mark Hopkins, other than he was an older, quiet, brooding man, whom Huntington had invited into the business after it was already established, and after both their stores had burned in one of the city's fires.

Ted took a deep reassuring breath of the cold night air, then strode confidently across the dirt street, dodging a dray loaded with rattling empty kegs of Jacob Grundlach Bavarian pulled by four stout gray horses.

When he mounted the boardwalk, Collis Huntington was just locking the front doors. He glanced up. "I thought you weren't coming," he said, sounding miffed.

Ted snatched the watch from his pocket and checked it. "Mine says seven on the nose."

"Good," Huntington said and stepped aside so Judah could enter. "I took the liberty of inviting a few others. They're already upstairs." Without turning back, he led Ted Judah to a stairway—threading their way through coils of rope, racks of pig iron, kegs of nails—then up, and through a glass-paneled door labeled Office.

Seven men stood or sat casually around the spacious but austere room. A partner's desk, a full six by six feet, was the predominate feature of the office—what you could see of it anyway for the papers stacked on top—and samples cluttered the walls and littered the floor. Four-drawer oak files lined one wall, and windows opened out facing K Street.

Huntington made the introductions. James Bailey, a jeweler, Ted already knew and considered a friend. Lewis Booth, a grocer; Charles Marsh, a miner from Nevada City; Charles Crocker, a dry-goods merchant; Horace Trimbly, a liveryman; and Baxter Willington, a freighter, all stepped forward to shake hands. The last to be introduced rose from his chair at the partner's desk. Mark Hopkins was a tall, austere, slightly sunken-cheeked man who reminded Ted of pictures he had seen of the new president, Abe Lincoln, only Hopkins was better looking. All of the men were well dressed and whiskered in one form or another.

In his normal brusque manner, Huntington got right to the point. "These fellows have their suppers waiting, Mr. Judah, and I smell a rain coming, so make your pitch." He settled in his chair across the partner's desk from Hopkins, dug a cigar from his waistcoat, and bit the end off.

The engineer in Ted Judah was a little offended by Huntington referring to his proposal as a "pitch," but he cleared his throat and began describing his background. Huntington stopped him short.

"I've already told these men, and most of them already knew, that you're well qualified to know if a road can be built, and what it should cost. Some of them were there last night. Get to the nitty-gritty." He clamped the cigar in his teeth.

"Thirty-five thousand dollars is the 'nitty-gritty,' gentlemen."

"And what will that buy us?" Mark Hopkins asked, speaking for the first time, his voice soft and his manner precise, but his brow deeply furrowed as he habitually stroked his long, thin beard.

"A survey."

"What good is a survey?" Hopkins asked flatly.

"A survey proves that a road can be built. You're all well aware of the proposed Railroad Act and what Congress is willing to do to see railroads constructed in this country . . . land grants, bonded participation."

"You're right," Huntington said. "We are all aware of the willingness of the politicians, though the 'Railroad Act' seems to have a lot of trouble coming to fruition . . . but that's not the nitty-gritty I speak of, Mr. Judah. The point is what kind of deal you're willing to make for the money. How much money, exactly, are *you* willing to invest in your project?"

"I've spent thousands of hours on this route and a good deal of time on this survey, Mr. Huntington. It's my skill and expertise—"

"You and your druggist friend from Dutch Flat," Huntington interrupted, his tone somewhat facetious. "We're all aware of that. But, to the point, what are you investing, and what are you willing to give up to get your money?"

"I'm investing my time, and my route . . . Doc Strong's and mine. You folks are investing the money."

Huntington, to Ted Judah's surprise, seemed satisfied at that. "Then you'll share and share alike with the founding contributors?"

"On an equitable basis," Ted said. "My partner, Doc Strong, included, of course."

"Of course," Huntington said and arose and walked across the room and extended his hand. "I'll come by the Tremont House tomorrow and tell you what we've decided."

"Fine," Ted said, shaking hands.

Huntington paused and took in the full glare of Mark Hopkins's cool eyes. "I'll tell you, Mr. Judah, we're about to have a problem in this country. As you well know, South Carolina has bolted from the Union in objection to Lincoln's election, and I think we're going to have some kind of major confrontation, maybe even a civil war. It's no time to be embarking on any kind of a speculative venture."

"All the more reason, sir, to bring the country that much closer together with a railroad over the Sierra, and it will also bring the free states of the West into the fold. Who knows, our road may reach all the way across the Mississippi . . . even tying up to Washington, D.C., someday."

"Uncle Mark," Huntington said, smiling, "let's discuss this without Mr. Judah." Many of Sacramento's younger men referred to Mark Hopkins, the senior among them at almost fifty years of age, as *uncle.*

This comment silenced the men. A railroad of that magnitude was certainly too much to contemplate. The gold fields of Nevada were one thing, but across the nation . . . Hell, Dutch Flat seemed halfway around the world when it came to railroading.

Ted stood for a moment in silence under the cold stares of the men, then realized he had been dismissed. He walked to a rack where he had parked his hat. Settled it on his head, adjusted it, then turned and nodded at the assemblage of men, who wished him a good evening. Huntington followed him down the stairs to let him out, but neither man said a word. Ted Judah tipped his hat and left.

As he made his way back to the Tremont, he did not know how to feel. *Good, I suppose,* he decided, but something niggled at him. It was his by-God route, and no one could take that away from him. He wondered what kind of a proposal they would come back to him with, if any. Probably these . . . these merchants . . . would want it all for themselves and want him to work for them for wages. Well, to hell with them. He would not do that. He would starve first.

With new dedication, he strode to the hotel in the growing cold, a fine misty rain occluding the few gas lights down K Street, girding himself for the many questions he knew Anna would ask and wishing he had answers for her.

After Judah had left, Collis Huntington led the discussion.

Horace Trimbly, the liveryman, and Baxter Willington, the freighter, left immediately, declaring that Theodore Judah's nickname of Crazy Judah had been well assigned.

Huntington turned to the others with a laugh after the two

had departed. "Old Horace doesn't like the thought of the iron horse replacing those flesh and blood horses he rents, and Baxter can't see far enough ahead to see that a growing California will ever need more feeder lines of horse-drawn freight wagons. All he can see is a railroad carrying a lot of freight that he might be carryin' otherwise."

"The timing is all wrong, Collis," Mark Hopkins said, shaking his head sagely.

"Think of this, Uncle Mark. A survey for a railroad will also work for a freight road. A toll road, connecting Sacramento all the way to Virginia City, the Hangtown route is raking in thousands in tolls. If that's all that comes of it, it'll be as good as the richest mine in the country."

"Judah wants a railroad," James Bailey, the jeweler, offered.

"You've been a friend of Judah's for a long time, Mr. Bailey," Huntington said in a placating manner. "I mean no disrespect to the man. His idea is a sound one, if a bit farfetched for those of us with limited means to contemplate. For a few merchants from Sacramento to try and build a railroad? . . . Let's take it a step at a time, and the survey is the first step. And if nothing else comes of it, then we'll have a fine route for a good wagon road."

They talked until the wee hours as the rain began pelting the roof in earnest, then, deciding it was not going to let up, took a quick vote and elected to provide Judah with the needed thirty-five thousand dollars, on the condition that there be seven shares. Judah and his partner could share one for the work they had done and could draw a modest salary for the work to be done.

With luck, and the grace of God, there would soon be a way across the formidable Sierra and, someday, a rail across the whole of this country.

"So, Pastor, how many men have you killed?" the youngster asked as Matt Preacher reclined in the shade, his blood trickling into the already red earth of Montana's Shoshoni Blood Canyon. Matt's voice was a little weak, so the boy hunkered down beside him.

Preacher, hair thick with salt and pepper before his time, coughed up a little blood and spat to the side, then let his cold, gray eyes settle on the boy, thinking a moment before he answered. "Don't matter," he finally said, his voice growing weaker.

"I think it matters. I truly think it matters a lot. Truly does matter to them what you shot dead." The boy seemed coldly intent but truly interested, then softened. "You want a drink of water?"

"Doc once told me if'n you was center shot, water's a bad thing. You can, however, take this kerchief from my neck and wet it, so I can give it a suck. My mouth is terrible dry. Spittin' salty blood don't help quench a thirst."

The boy complied, walking to the trickle that worked its way out of the red rock cliffs above where they'd found some shade in a copse of cottonwood. He brought the soaked rag back and handed it to Matt, who sucked some sustenance and relief from its wetness.

"So, how many?" the boy persisted.

"Stopped counting at a dozen or so . . ."

"All sinners?" the boy pressed.

"We're all sinners, son, just some worse than others." Matt chuckled, then coughed.

"Was it killin' men what brought you to the pulpit?"

He chuckled again and, as before, coughed. "No, son, it was the pulpit what brought me to killin'. My ma gave me this Biblical name, Matthew, and, of course, my pa cursed me with the Preacher half, took our surname serious as road-apple-round hail on a wheat crop, and taught me the Bible front to back and then back to front, 'til I could recite it—at least a fair chunk of it—word for word. With a name like Matthew Preacher, and a Pa a man of the cloth, I was destined . . . maybe damned."

"And you believed every word the book said?" the boy asked. He'd been with Matt Preacher two days, and now that Matt was flat on his back, near center shot, it was the first time he'd had the bravery to question the man known as Pastor Matthew Preacher, particularly to those who came to his wagon when he rode his circuit through Montana, some of Wyoming, and a touch of Idaho. He said he was known by other names to those who feared retribution for their sins, but they weren't handles he favored. Some of those handles, like Reaper, were gained as he hunted men at the same time he was travelling the circuit saving souls. He often said it was tit for tat.

It took even longer for him to answer the question about believing. It seemed as if on the precipice of death, he wanted to make sure he was telling the youth the right path. Finally, he gathered enough want to answer, "My pa believed it a sacrilege not to embrace every word. I believe every word was written with good intent, every word with good purpose, every word written so, later, it could be used to bring some contentment to those who doubt every word or any of what was written. Much of it is hyperbole, which is forgiven when trying to save men's souls."

"Hy what?"

"Exaggeration."

"Oh. How about thou shalt not kill? I wouldn't think the pulpit would bring you to that."

Matt coughed again and spat a little blood, then cleared his throat with a hack before he continued. "Ain't what the original script said."

"That's the way I heard it for all my sixteen years."

"Well, it's taught wrong; in fact, I've been guilty of teaching it wrong."

"So, what's right?"

"Thou shalt not *murder* is what's right. And I believe that with all my heart and soul. I put stress on the eye for eye, tooth for tooth recitation."

The boy rose from kneeling on his haunches and crossed again to the creek. He dropped to his chest and sucked water, then rose and returned, the front of his shirt wet.

Matt eyed him with concern. "You might hang that shirt in the sun for a while. It could get truly cold tonight."

"I will." The boy unbuttoned the shirt and hung it on a nearby marionberry bush that was yet to be stripped clean by the bears. Then he again hunkered down next to Matt. "You think they'll come back?"

"They think they finished me and probably are right . . . and don't give a hoot about you, I wouldn't guess. Besides, the way you shoot, they likely don't want to mess with you." He managed a smile, and the boy returned it. Preacher continued, "Let's hope they ride on to Helena . . . or, hell, Texas would be fine."

"Let's hope. How come you're hunting this bohunk, Kabowski?"

Matt took a deep breath, then winced with pain. "First man I ever killed rode with Slippery Jack Kabowski and his gang of owlhoots."

"Why'd you kill that one?"

"He shot my pa."

"He, Kabowski, or the man what rode with him?"

"Kabowski. I was your age, and Kabowski was only about four years older. He's a half-breed—half-Shawnee, half-Polack—riverboat cutthroat. This was two decades ago, a'fore the war. And way back on the banks of the Ohio River. I had to shoot his sidekick to get at him, but he hightailed it. Can you help me sit up against this tree trunk?"

"Yes, sir," the boy said, hooking a hand under Matt's arm and pulling while Matt pushed with his legs and other hand. The boy watched him for a long moment while Matt leaned against the cottonwood with his eyes tightly shut and his mouth drawn so tight he had snake lips. "You okay?" the boy asked.

Matt cleared his throat again. "I thought I was sure dead, but now I have a hankerin' to live as I seem to be getting some air from time to time—at least live long enough to gut shoot Kabowski and watch him bleed out, slow like. He rode with some fellas I caught up with over Virginia City way. They paid for their foul deeds, but Kabowski wasn't with them. I've been tracking him."

"And that's not murder? Those four you say you shot down?" the boy asked, doubt in voice and eyes.

"Why, hell no, boy. I never committed a murder. Ever' man who fell under my gun was wanted by the law and wouldn't come along peaceable, or was in the process of doing something heinous."

The boy seemed to weigh that a few moments, then asked, "Should I be worrying about supper?"

Matt managed a smile. "If I live the night, I'm liable to be a bother to you for a long while after. These wounds will take a good while to heal."

"Then I should worry about supper?"

"You should worry about yourself. Like I said, if'n I live the night, I won't be taking any food for a while, neither way." He managed a tight smile.

"We passed a cabin down a quarter mile into the trees from the river before those cowards dry-gulched you. Least I figure it a cabin, as they was a wisp of stove pipe or chimney smoke . . ."

"Wasn't exactly dry-gulched. They rode right up face to face." Then Matt Preacher turned white, closed his eyes, and knotted his jaw as if someone had driven a knife in and twisted. He grasped his stomach with both hands, covering the lower wound. One .44 slug had passed through him just below the rib cage on the right side, and another just below the collarbone on the left, probably nicking the high side of a lung. Either wound would likely kill him. He let his arms slide to his sides, looked up at the boy, gave him a whisper of a smile, then his head slumped, and he didn't move. But the boy thought he heard the rattle of low breathing.

The boy reached over and pressed a hand to Matt's neck, seeing if he could find a pulse. He believed he did, so he rose and headed into the brush where he'd hidden the horses.

He gathered up the strawberry roan gelding the pastor had let him ride, saddled him with the preacher's saddle rather than the packsaddle he'd been sitting, and headed south back the way they'd come. Preacher's blood bay jerked his picket pin and followed. The boy dismounted, removed the halter and lead rope from the bay, and let him trail along, running free.

Preacher had come down the trail two days after the boy's ma and pa had been killed by a Crow band while the boy was afoot, up in the timber, looking for a fat doe for the pot. Luckily the savages were yelling in victory as he neared the wagon road. The sight he came upon—a fierce Indian with half his face painted red and half black over his mother—was one that would never leave him, and he'd had nightmares since. They'd burned the wagon and drove off the two yokes of oxen. Oxen now likely jerky. The boy carried a thirty-caliber muzzleloader, older than his own sixteen years by twice. It was all he could do not to fire into the group of a dozen savages but knew it sure death if he did, so he slipped away and stayed hidden in a heavy stand of chokecherries until they tired of looting and rode away, whooping and hollering, leaving his ma and pa naked, fileted, and gutted like pigs and forcing him to keep his eyes closed while dragging them to the shallow graves he'd been able to dig with the broken shovel left by the savages. It took him more than a day to bury them and mark their graves.

Riding on as he contemplated the fate of his folks, he, for the hundredth time, swore he'd find that band of Crow and take revenge.

It was no more than two miles before he again saw a tendril of smoke working its way up out of a stand of lodgepole pine, and he gigged the roan that way. Soon, a cabin appeared, its back dug into a sagebrush-spotted sandstone cliff, only two shuttered windows and a door facing out. And they, he noted, had slots for rifle barrels. The forest in front had been cleared away in a semicircle for almost a hundred feet, stumps still showing. He eyed the place and figured whoever had constructed it had done so from the lodgepole pines cleared. The uppermost of the pines had been used as rafters, side nestled to side and covered with sod, the lower used for the log house. Grass grew six inches deep on the roof, so it had been there at least this season. More than two dozen fruit trees—no older than five years—formed an orchard north of the cabin. An outbuilding, probably a barn with no more than four stalls, sat fifty feet back and south next to the lodgepole, a small corral extending from it across a trickle of water that worked its way out of a buckbrush-lined cleft in the sandstone cliff.

The boy reined up fifty feet from the plank front door, both the roan and the bay dropped their heads and began grazing, and he called out, "Hello, the house."

Waiting the count of ten, he shouted louder, "Hello, the house!"

In a moment, the door opened just an inch or two. He gigged the horse closer, then a shout rang out through the crack, "I'm going to shoot," and he gulped deeply and wondered if he dared run.

"That's close enough, young stranger. State your business."

It was a woman's voice, so he understood her reticence in flinging the door aside. Owlhoots like Slippery Jack Kabowski had been roaming the land for a long while, not to speak of the bloodthirsty Crow, Sioux, Shoshoni, Blackfoot, and other tribes. And, even worse, half-breeds like those who rode with Kabowski. The massacre at Greasy Grass, or the Little Big Horn as the papers called it, was only a year past, and the savages were emboldened.

The boy lifted his head to yell in return, "Ma'am, I'm riding with a circuit preacher, and he's been shot bad down the trail a ways. He needs doctorin' real bad, and to lay up a spell to see if he's goin' to meet his maker or get healed up."

The door opened slowly. The woman was young, not so young as he, but still fresh and attractive in a homesteader sort of way. The apron she wore was tight enough to see she had an hourglass shape somewhere beneath the gingham dress that swept the floor wherever she moved. The sunbonnet cupped a face that would cause any man to gulp deeply and be momentarily dumbfounded. More impressive to the boy, she held a Golden Boy Henry, but its muzzle was lowered so as not to insult an honest visitor. A child of no more than four or five clung to her skirt, its face buried in the folds. Probably a boy child, as it was clad in pants made of flour sacks, although it wore a linsey-woolsey shirt that could have been store bought.

The woman seemed to sigh deeply before she spoke. "Tie your horse over to the trough, and come on in. I've got a buckboard over in the barn. If you can work the harness to those two critters you brought, we can go fetch him soon as I get this baby dressed for the weather what's coming."

"I never harnessed these two. You got no wagon stock?"

"Sad to say, no. The no-goods ran off with them. Would have taken me, too, and left Davy to fend for himself, had I not had friend Henry here. We got to use your stock, if you want to fetch the preacher back here flat on his back. Otherwise, he's a horsebacker, and it sounds like that just might finish him."

The boy eyed the sky, clean as a virgin's dream, and wondered where she got her information about the weather— but didn't challenge her.

Instead, he reined the strawberry over to the trough, dismounted, and ground tied him as there was no rail, letting him drink. The bay followed.

He had one of the pastor's lever-action rifles in a saddle boot but thought twice about slipping it out to take inside. He didn't want the woman to fret.

She greeted him with a bowl of venison stew, laced with carrots and potatoes, a chunk of thick bread, and a glass of buttermilk, and he could barely keep from grinning as he sat at her table and wolfed it down. He figured he couldn't serve the preacher well were he starving to death. He'd need his strength to haul him back.

She managed to inform him, between slurps of stew and broth, "They purloined the horses and our plow mule, but I had the milk cow up in a pasture above the cliff, staked out and grazing, so we still have her and her bounty, thank the good Lord."

As he mopped up the last of the juice from the bowl, he rose. "Obliged for the sustenance, ma'am. Right delicious. I got to go back and see to him."

"Harness up those two horses you brought. He's still alive, so let's hurry."

"How do you know he's still alive?" the boy looked at her, his brows furrowed.

"I know. Things come to me since . . . since we had a death in the family. Important things, at least. Let's go." She turned to the child. "Pull your knit hat on, Davy. It's cooling down out there. It's gonna snow tonight."

The boy stared at her again. "Snow? Why, it ain't even cloudy."

"It's gonna snow. Let's go. If we don't get him back here pronto, he's sure not going to make it."

She followed, cradling the rifle under an arm with an easy familiarity. Close behind the boy, she led the bay while he trailed the strawberry roan to the barn. She worked right along with him, seeming to know the harness better than most hostlers. They had the pair rigged up in no time. The child rode in the back of the buckboard, the woman on the left, and he drove, whipping up the stock.

As they moved away, she asked, "I suppose you got a name?"

"Yes, ma'am. Thaddeus."

"Just one?"

"No, ma'am. Thaddeus Arthur Allenthorp."

"And I am Mrs. Tobias McCallister. You may call me Rose."

"Yes'm," Thad said.

The horses fought each other for the first mile, then settled into stride, and, before long, he pulled rein.

"Mrs. Rose . . ."

"Just Rose is fine."

"Yes, ma'am. He's up that draw, just below the cut in the cliff. We can't get the rig up there, but you and I can get him down, with luck . . . if'n he's still alive."

"He's alive. Let's go."

The boy was surprised the way she sprang from the buckboard wearing skirts to her ankles. The youngster started to climb down, but she scolded him. "You stay, Davy. Mind the team." She handed him the reins, which surprised Thad, as the child couldn't be more than five. "We'll be less than ten minutes."

"He's a mite young . . ." Thad started to say but was interrupted.

"Necessity makes us all grow quickly out here," she said.

"Dang if it don't," Thad replied.

"Watch your tongue, young man."

"Yes'm."

To Thad's great surprise, Preacher was still breathing when they got to him. With some trouble they hoisted him to his feet, and, with an arm over each of their shoulders with him mumbling a passage from the Bible—something about a valley and the shadow of death—they soon had him at the rear of the buckboard. Thad threw the tailgate aside, and they laid him face down, his legs extending a foot beyond. Both of them climbed into the back of the buckboard and dragged him, moaning low, up until fully inside. Then with the boy whipping up the team, they headed at a rattling trot back to the cabin.

She finally asked him, "What did you say your name was?"

"Thaddeus. Friends call me Thad. Thaddeus Arthur Allenthorp. And you're Mrs. McCallister."

"Rose."

"Yes, ma'am. And the boy?"

"David, like his pa. Davy will do fine. Then Thad it is. And the preacher?"

"Preacher."

"Yes, the preacher; what's his name?"

The boy laughed. "Fact is, his name is Preacher. Pastor Matthew Preacher . . . said he didn't have much choice as to his calling."

Her brow furrowed. "I've heard of him. Some call him the Reaper."

"I hadn't heard that."

"It's a fact. He killed four men over in Virginia City for the bounty on them and, the way I heard it, didn't give them much chance."

"They was wanted men?"

"Yes, they were wanted men. But that doesn't always mean a man needs killing. A man is entitled to a fair trial, judged by his peers."

The boy thought on that for a moment. "What were they wanted for?"

"Robbing a bank in Helena."

"That's all . . . just robbing?"

"Don't say 'just robbing.' That was folks' hard-earned savings they ran off with. Folks could starve without their savings, or even die of heartbreak due to them taking what wasn't theirs to have. Folks may have worked years for that savings. Anyway, they shot down a teller, and, when firing back at the sheriff, a youngster, no older than Davy, got gut shot and, the way I heard it, took a hard week to die."

"Then Preacher did right, killing those four."

She shook her head. "I wish I was as sure as you."

"A youngster suffered and died hard."

"But only one of them fired the shot."

"But they was all . . . how do you say that word . . . the preacher used it the other day . . . they was all calculable."

"Culpable. They were all culpable. All at fault."

"That's it. Culpable. Did the money get back to the folks and the bank?"

"Not that I know of. But I only hear from folks on occasion, so don't rightly know."

With some trouble, they got Preacher inside the cabin just as the bats began to fly and gather moths out of the failing light. They put him, head hanging and Thad holding him up, in a bentwood river-willow chair while she made a pallet of blankets and a goose down comforter in front of the hearth. Then they lowered him there. He wakened just long enough to grunt a "thank you" and then fell into what was more than mere sleep—likely a coma. She cut his shirt away and threw the bloody rags in the fire, cleaned his wounds, poured a shot of whiskey in each, then stitched them closed on the front—the entry side—but could only stuff and bind the exit side. Each exit wound was the size of half her fist.

"He's still breathing," Thad said, and she nodded.

"If he makes it through the night, I'll get some broth down him." She turned to Thad. "You fetch a couple or three armloads of firewood from the side of the cabin. We'll want to keep him warm tonight."

After he'd loaded the woodbin, next to the hearth, to overflowing, she waved him back to the table. "I got a couple of slices left from the last pie . . ."

"You bet," he said, before she could finish.

As he and the child devoured the pie, she sat with a cup of thick coffee and eyed him. Then when he'd finished the last bite and thanked her for the third time, she asked, "Is Preacher your pa or an uncle or something?"

He shook his head. "No, ma'am. I was hiding along the trail . . ."

"Hiding from what?"

"I don't much care to talk about it."

Her voice became stern. "Young man, you want me to shelter you and share our crumbs, you'll fess up."

He took a deep breath, then began. "My ma and pa and I

85

come all the way from St. Joseph, turning north off the Oregon Trail at Laramie, headed for the mining territory in Idaho where Pa hoped to start a mercantile, when a band of savages come at us."

"How did you escape?"

"I was up the mountain side, afoot, trying to down a fat doe we'd spotted, and they didn't know my presence. When I heard the ruckus and got back in sight of the wagon, they'd already . . . already . . ." He cut his eyes away, and she could see he was tearing up. Then he turned back, anger in his tone. "One of them was an ugly lout with his face painted half red and half black. I'll never forget him or what he did to my ma."

"His name is Red Hawk. He burned out a ranch over in the next valley and did lots more. There's five hundred dollars on his head."

"Damn his ugly hide," Thad said, then choked up and sobbed a time or two.

"That's all right, Thad. I know of the atrocities. So, you hid out?"

"After I cared for my folks . . . or what was left of them."

"Hard task," she said, laying a hand on his shoulder.

"I did hide out, staying in the woods but in sight of the road. I was there that night and one more before I saw Preacher coming down the trail, leading a pack horse."

"So, how'd Preacher get those wounds?"

"We hadn't gone half a day when he saw riders coming our way, and he shooed me off into the brush. He gave me his Winchester and shoved my old muzzleloader into the scabbard. Those fellas—Preacher said Jack Kabowski was the leader—saw it was Preacher from fifty yards away and went to galloping right at him and shooting. And they was six of them."

"There were six, you mean."

"But Preacher didn't run. Instead he spurred his horse,

hunkered down, and filled a hand with his six-gun. I saw him jerk, then jerk again as they fired at him. Four of them wheeled their horses and headed for the brush, but two followed as Preacher reined off and gave heels to his roan. He sagged in the saddle as they came into the trees, and his horse clomped to a stop with him lying across the roan's neck. Them two fellas—"

"Those two . . ."

"Yes, ma'am. Those two fellas reined up beside him, laughing, watching him bleed. I couldn't stand it, and from seventy-five yards or so, I lay down on them with the Winchester just as one cocked his pistol and aimed to shoot Preacher in the head."

"And?"

"And that one of them was knocked right out of his saddle, and the other one had to control his mount, as it was doing a fancy bunch of humps. I think I hit him as well as he finally got control but jerked in the saddle, then hunkered down and rode away. I wasted no time, galloped down, and gathered up Preacher's reins, and we lit out more than two miles 'till I feared Preacher was dead and found some deep timber to get him down out of the saddle. That's where we—you and me—went back to find him."

"And Jack Kabowski?"

"I don't know which one he was. But they didn't follow, at least not right away. They likely are still licking their wounds somewheres."

"Somewhere. Kabowski is a bearded lout."

"Yes, ma'am. More'n one of them had face hair."

"Jack Kabowski knows this place. It was him and his worthless bunch that shot my David dead and stole my stock. I truly hope it was him you shot dead."

"Fellow I shot was near clean shaven, only a week's stubble. Seemed to me you didn't hold much with killing?"

"Men, no. Vermin, yes; and Kabowski is vermin."

"Throat dry . . ." the sound came from the pallet, a rasping moan.

Rose jumped up, wet a rag in a white porcelain bowl, then filled a tin mug and hurried over and kneeled at Preacher's side. She wet his lips with the rag, then asked, "You want to try and drink some water . . . maybe some broth?"

"Pour a little water in my mouth, please," he whispered, and she did.

He choked and coughed, then cried out. "By damn . . . sorry. Can't cough."

"I'm sure not," she said. "You want to try some broth?"

But he didn't answer, and his breathing deepened.

She got back to her feet, took the child by the hand, and turned to Thad. "Since David left us, Davy has been sleeping with me. You can take his bed in the loft."

"Night, Davy," Thad said, and the child waved over his shoulder as he headed for the next room. Then Thad smiled and called after Rose. "He don't say much, does he?"

She stopped and gave him a sad smile. "He hasn't spoken a word since he saw his father shot down. I hope he'll come back to being himself soon. God willing."

"Yes'm," Thad said and watched her disappear into the next room. The cabin was two rooms with a ladder leading up to a loft over what he presumed was her bedroom. A vegetable cellar was dug back into the hill, covered by a plank door. Only one of the windows and the door was in the main room; the other he'd seen from outside must be in her room.

Thad took a peek into the vegetable cellar before he headed for the ladder. It was nearly ten feet deep and wide enough to be lined with shelves on both sides. He smiled to see her stores: canned peaches, apples, green beans, applesauce, and tomatoes. A couple of large smoked hams and two sides of bacon hung to one side. Two small butter churns rested in a corner, next to a sack of flour, one of salt, and one of dry beans. They wouldn't starve, he thought with a smile, then headed for the ladder to find his accommodations.

Rose perched herself on the edge of her bed and watched her child undress and don his nightshirt. As he did, she wondered how she had come to this? Her husband of only seven years moldering in a cold grave; a strange man in her house, severely wounded, who would likely die—a man whose reputation was somewhere between heaven and hell; and a strange boy who claimed he was recently orphaned by savages and who shot dead a shooter of the man known as Preacher and, more ominously, as Reaper. She shook her head in wonderment and awe. And to think less than a decade ago she'd been a teacher with a warm whitewashed home and one-room school in Altoona, Pennsylvania. Now, where was life to lead her?

One thing she was sure of, the men who'd killed her husband and rode off with her stock would likely be back. She'd invited a man and boy into their home whom they had a grudge against, a man who seemed like a magnet for trouble. And a boy who'd recently made them an enemy as well.

She knew for sure that she'd pick up the gun should any of them threaten her son.

She had her son to protect and knew she'd done the Christian thing by taking the man in and tending to his injuries. But, the Christian thing could get her son in a cold grave next to her husband. She worried little about herself, but her son . . . her son was her all and all she had left in the world, and already deeply wounded, struck dumb by the violence done his father. She knew that wounds to the soul were many times worse than wounds to the body.

She sighed deeply, and it was a long time before she slipped into the warmth and safety of sleep, for every night sound seemed to be murderers and thieves slipping up on the cabin.

She awoke with the first chattering of a flicker working a nearby pine and decided to go ahead and shock her houseguests by pulling on a pair of trousers and a flannel shirt, pants and shirt that had belonged to her husband that she couldn't afford to let go to waste. The boy, Thad, was already awake and had stoked the fire in both her cast-iron stove and the fireplace. She smiled at him.

"Thank you for taking care of the fires . . . and good morning."

"Morning, ma'am."

"And Mr. Preacher?"

"Awake in the night and bothered me for a drink, but quiet since. Still suckin' in a breath so maybe some better. You were right, by the way."

"Right?"

"We got a dusting of snow last night, but the clouds are broken, and I'm sure it'll melt off."

"It will, but we need to worry about winter. Are you good with ax and saw?"

"Yes, ma'am. I'll have the wood bin overflowing given a little time."

She opened the door to the vegetable cellar and soon was handing Thad a bucket. "You know how to milk a cow?"

" 'Course I do. And I suppose fork her a bit of hay?"

"And your horses. We have a corral above the bluff, more than an acre of meadow grass with a trickle of water if you'd like to lead them up. There's a track about fifty good paces to the south beyond the barn. I'd imagine you'd be able to handle that task . . . and a stack of flapjacks when you're done? You saw the privy?"

"Done been out that way," Thad said. "Any other chores?"

"There're a dozen hens in the pen you can let have the run of the place, and check for eggs. Should be at least a half dozen. Don't turn your back on that old red rooster. He'll try to spur you."

"Yes, ma'am."

"Hurry along. Flapjacks will take no time."

"Ma'am." It was the raspy rattle of Preacher's voice.

The boy hurried out as she went to the wounded man's side. "Your eyes are bright and clear, Mr. Preacher. That's a good sign."

"Stiff. Feel like I was run over by a freight wagon."

She pulled down his cover and checked his wounds. "I believe you have not bled from any of these holes. I don't imagine you need the chamber pot?"

"Not yet. Seems my body is done dried out, but thanks for asking. Besides, the boy can tend to those kind of needs if'n you don't mind."

"Mr. Preacher . . ."

"Matt, if you would, ma'am."

"Matt. Matt, I tended soldiers at the end of the war when I was but fourteen years old. I tended folks with cholera and yellow fever. When it comes to nursing there's not much I haven't seen, including the sawing off of limbs. Modesty is best left on the shelf when it comes to nursing. Besides," she laughed, "you're not comely enough to be vain."

They both laughed, and Preacher winced and held his side, with her teasing.

For the first time since she'd seen him, he managed the small smile and chuckle. "Kind of you to notice and comment . . . still, if the boy's around . . . By the way, where is the boy?"

91

"Chores. Would you like a sip of water before I get to mine?"

"Don't mind if I do." And she obliged.

It was three days before he could sit up, and another day before he asked for privacy and the boy to help him with the chamber pot. At least his body was beginning to work again. After a week he was eating, and on the tenth day, he'd managed to get on his feet and, with the boy's help, out to the privy.

As they took the slow walk back to the cabin, Preacher asked him, "No sign of Slippery Jack or the Crow or any other trouble?"

"No, sir. Had a bear down, black bear I think, but I run him off. Think he was admiring the chickens."

Preacher gave him a smile. "Dang if you're not handy as a pocket in a shirt. I'm gonna owe you, boy, when I get afoot again."

"You plucked me outta the woods, Mr. Preacher. I'll owe you for a month of Sundays for that kind deed."

Just as they reached the cabin door, the horses, still in the small barn, began acting up. They neighed loudly, and Preacher and Thad stopped on the porch and listened. As they expected, a distant neigh answered.

"Inside," Preacher snapped. As soon as he shut the door behind, he yelled to Rose, who was drying the breakfast dishes. "Someone coming. Suggest you get the boy in the cellar. I noticed a scattergun in your room. How about passing that to me."

She quickly grabbed Davy by the hand, shoved him into the cave that served as a cellar, hurried to her room, and returned with both the Henry and a twelve-gauge coach gun. She handed it over and cautioned, "A tinker, Mr. Rosenberg, calls about this time each month. Don't be shooting an innocent man."

"I got no hankering to kill a tinsmith." He turned to Thad.

"My Colt is hanging on the hat rack over yonder. Fetch it and my Winchester and take the slot in Rose's window." Then he turned to Rose. "Stick your barrel out the other window slot. Even if you don't favor shootin' some owlhoot, the barrel might dissuade some trouble."

"Some stranger, not likely, Slippery Jack, no problem."

"If you don't mind, I'll let you do the talking, should talking be necessary. Might be some advantage if my presence remains a surprise."

They all stood at the gunports, silently, for a long while, nearly an hour, until Rose finally spoke up. "You sure you heard a horse approach."

Before Preacher could answer, they heard footsteps, not outside but on the sod roof.

"Douse those fires. They mean to smoke us out," Preacher snapped, and Rose left her post and hurriedly watered the stove and fireplace down. As Preacher predicted, smoke began to creep out of the fireplace but luckily not enough to bother.

It was another fifteen minutes before a voice rang out from the timber line, over a hundred feet away. "Hello in there! Y'all got a little water to share with a friendly and thirsty traveler?"

Preacher gave Rose a nod, and she answered. "It would be a traveler lower than dog dung who'd block the chimney and try and smoke folks out. Step on out, so I can get a look at the lowlife."

"That's not very neighborly, missy."

"Neither is trying to smoke us like a side of bacon."

"We tracked a fella thisaway. One who took a few shots at us a fortnight ago. Why don't you send him on out, and we'll be on our way?"

Rose's voice lowered an octave. "Mister, I don't know who or what you're blabbin' on about, but it's just me and my youngster in here."

"And them two horses in the barn? Last time we was hereabout, that barn was empty."

"It was, thanks to some lowlife scum-suckin' pigs who drove my stock off. I don't guess you'd know anything about that?"

"So, missy, where'd those two critters come from? Godsent, I guess."

"You'd guess right. They wandered in. I grained them and stalled them, and I plan to keep them. Henry here said I could."

"Henry?" the voice was questioning.

"Yes, sir."

"I thought it was just you and your young'un?"

"Henry would be happy to have a talk with you, should you step out in the open and stop playing the cowardly dog."

He was silent for a moment, then his voice also deepened, and he growled, "That's mighty amusing. I'd guess Henry is the yellow one."

"You'd guess right. Step on out."

"Okay, boys!" he shouted.

Shots, almost as one, splintered the shutters and door, and the three of them inside moved aside to be protected by the thick lodgepole logs. Shots thumped into the thick logs as well, causing no damage other than dust motes floating down from the sod roof.

Preacher shushed them with a finger to his lips, then whispered, "Let them think they killed us with that first volley."

"How'd you like that fine howdy, missy?" the voice rang out again. Only this time, she stayed silent, and none of them pushed a barrel through the gunports.

"Hey, the cabin!" the voice rang out even louder. "You need a little doctorin' in there?"

Still, she remained silent.

Preacher whispered again. "Don't show a barrel until at least three of them are out in the clear. Let them come—close as twenty paces—so this coach gun can do its job."

Both Rose and Thad nodded at him.

It was at least five minutes of silence, which seemed an hour, before one of them stepped into the open.

"Move on out there, Scroggins," another voice rang out, and the man in the clear walked another twenty feet closer to the cabin.

"Closer," the second voice commanded.

"Bugger yourself, Jack," the man in the clear said, then yelled, "Hello, the cabin. I mean y'all no harm."

That made Rose snicker but nearly silently.

After another few seconds, four more men slipped out of the copse of trees, each of them several paces apart.

"I'll be taking the middle one," Rose whispered. "That's Slippery Jack."

Preacher returned her whisper. "I was saving him for myself," he said with a snicker. "Just don't miss."

He waited a moment, then continued, "I'll count down from three when they're close enough." Preacher still whispered. He watched through his gunport, but all three of them stayed far enough back to cast no movement that could be seen from the approaching five men. Then, to their surprise, two red men stepped from the trees and followed closely. One of them had a face painted half red, half black.

The boy gasped deeply, then mumbled. "That's him, that's the one scalped my ma, and worse." He raised Preacher's lever action, and Preacher barely got to him before he shoved the weapon through the barrel slot.

"Wait," Preacher commanded. "You wait to show that barrel until I count down."

The boy glared at him, his jaw knotted, but he nodded.

It was less than fifteen seconds when Preacher began his countdown. "Three. Two. One."

Then he shouted, "Fire!" and the three of them shot almost as one. Then the shotgun's second barrel fired, and both Rose and Thad levered in another shell, and each fired twice more.

Shots were returned, again splintering and blowing holes in doors and shutters. They ducked aside, then Preacher quickly returned to the slot but had to wait for gun smoke to clear to see the results or pick another target.

Three men were on the ground, a fourth and fifth were crawling back toward the trees.

"Rose, shoot those men trying to crawl away."

"I can't. They're wounded and out of the fight."

Preacher ran over and wrenched the Henry out of her hands, levered in another shot, but, before he could fire, Thad's rifle bucked in the boy's hands, and one of those crawling, an Indian, rolled to his back and stilled. Preacher swung his muzzle to the other man, fired, and the man jerked but kept crawling, now on his stomach. Preacher fired again, and the man rolled to his back and kicked a few times but stilled.

Preacher stepped away from the slot, just as another chunk of lead blew splinters out and holed the door again. He leaned against the logs and breathed deeply for a moment, then smiled tightly at Rose.

"I believe we have prevailed. That hooligan in the red shirt and suspenders is Slippery Jack, and if I saw correctly, you ventilated his breastbone with your first shot. The boy gave Mister Red Hawk a stomachache with his first and cured it with the next two. He'll not have another ache until he's in Hell."

"And you?" Rose asked.

"My loads each took out a man. It seems there were seven of them, now down to maybe only two, and they may be discouraged with a hole or two in their hide."

"Mama," a small voice called out from the now-open door to the cellar cave.

"Davy, you get back in there."

"Is the bad man dead?"

"Davy, the man who shot your pa will not hurt anyone, ever again." She ran over and took the child up in her arms. Then she turned to Matt. "Mr. Preacher . . ."

"Matt, remember."

"Matt, I'm sorry, but my wrath was spent as soon as I saw Kabowski tumble and knew he was on his way to meet his maker."

"Doubt that, ma'am. He's going the other way to meet the hot bed of Hell."

"From your lips to God's ears."

"How many do you think are left out there?" Preacher asked.

"I don't know."

"I thought you had the gift?"

"I did. I think the good Lord granted me something special when I needed it, and it seems I no longer do."

"And I hope you never need it again. What now?" he asked.

"Let's wait awhile to let those other two decide it would be healthier down in Wyoming or somewhere."

Preacher gave her a tight smile. "I do believe they are properly discouraged. I heard a couple of horses pounding trail like their tails were a'fire. Then what?" he asked.

Her look turned serious. "Well, if it suits you, and if you're up to it, I think we ought to give what's left of those worthless louts a taste of hell right here?"

"Ma'am?" Thad asked, while Preacher waited for her to explain.

She took a deep breath before continuing. "This is no place for a woman alone to try and raise a son. If you'd see me back to Virginia City, I believe I could make a living sewing and baking, and they might need a schoolmarm."

Preacher cleared his throat. "A taste of hell?"

"Yes, sir. I won't be needing this cabin, and it has lots of bad memories. I say we load up the wagon with what I can take, then load up the cabin with those louts and put the torch to it. It's not ladylike, but it won't offend my sensitivity to ride away with the lot of them cooking in our own version of hellfire."

Preacher couldn't help but smile. "Dang sight easier than digging a half-dozen holes, and my diggin' days are over for a while at least."

"Agreed. You'll see me back to town?"

Preacher turned to Thad. "Load up that magazine, and I'll top off this Henry. You and I are going to go reconnoiter this battlefield and make sure what's left of the enemy have yielded the field."

"Yes, Captain," Thad said, a wide grin following his words.

They slipped out into the noonday sun staying as silent as possible, then went from man to man, making sure that each was dead. To their surprise, Red Hawk still breathed shallowly.

"He's worth a pile of money," Preacher said. "Your money. You downed the Hawk."

"That money, dead or alive?" Thad asked.

"Yep, either way."

Thad knelt by the big Indian and reached down with both hands, one covering the man's mouth, one pinching his nose shut. He glanced up at Preacher while he worked. "I do believe my ma and pa are smiling down on me, no matter how heinous this work. Do you think that a hyperbole?"

"I think it proper to say 'do I think that hyperbole,' not a hyperbole . . . but no, I do not."

Preacher made no move to stop him; rather, he scratched his head and mumbled, "Damn if he didn't make you angry."

Thad merely nodded and stayed in position until the Indian stopped shifting from side to side, then stilled, forever.

"How long to Virginia City and the law?" Thad asked, standing and brushing his hands together as if to rid himself of the Indian.

"Three days, driving the wagon."

"Good. This animal stinks already, and we need to get him there in a hurry to prove our claim."

"Your claim. There's bound to be some horses tied up out in the timber. How about you being real stealthy and take a look? Be careful; there's enough fellas shot for one day."

"I'll be like a shadow."

Preacher returned to the cabin to find Rose on her knees, hugging Davy.

"He's talking just fine," Preacher said, giving them both a wide grin.

"Thank God. Killing came to some good end."

"Ended some bad fellas, that's for sure." Preacher sank to a knee beside them. "Ma'am, I don't see any reason for you to have to take to sewing and baking once we get to Virginia City."

"Sir?"

"Last time I passed through, a friend of mine, the sheriff there, offered me a job as deputy, and the Baptist church there is in need of a pastor. I do believe that both jobs would pay enough to support you and Davy."

"Why, Matt Preacher, if I didn't know better, I'd think that a proposal!"

"You know just fine. Would it be okay if Thad bunked with us until he reached his majority?"

"I haven't said *yes*, yet."

"Yes," little Davy said and giggled.

"I guess that settles it," Rose said, and the three of them hugged, on their knees, on the dirt floor of a cabin destined to soon become a pyre.

They arose, and Rose dusted off the trousers she wore. Then she said, "I don't suppose you'll give up the gospel of the gun and take on the gospel of the word?"

"I'll do my very best to oblige. But no one knows better than you, this is a hard land. I got to check on Thad."

When he walked out of the cabin Thad was approaching, leading a dappled gray, a piebald Indian pony, and a fine looking palomino.

"Seems you caught up some wild horses," Preacher said with a laugh.

"Dang if I didn't. And two of them with saddles and bridles, can you imagine that?"

"Hard to fathom. We got to help the lady get some goods out of the cabin, then load it with all this suet."

"All except old red and black face. We need to trade him in for a reward."

"We'll do that. Then we got a celebration to attend."

"It ain't the Fourth of July?"

"Not hardly. You ever been the best man in a wedding?"

No Irish Need Apply

Dutch Flat, California
October 1860

The small sign in the window under the much larger gold-gilded sign, Rosco Pugh's Saloon, was crudely lettered, but Sean McKenna had no trouble reading it.

HELP WANTED
PUGH FREIGHTING & WHOLESALE LIQUOR
INQUIRE INSIDE
NO IRISH NEED APPLY

He had two dollars to his name. The last thing he needed to waste his money on was a shot of whiskey or mug of ale, but this time, he could not resist.

His muddy brogans, so thin he could feel the grain of the wood underfoot, rang on the boardwalk as he moved to the batwing doors and shoved his way inside. Two dozen or more miners, bullwhackers, and drovers lounged in the dingy saloon. Like most of them, Sean carried a Colt strapped to his hip, a .31-caliber pocket model he'd won in a poker game. Smoke clung to the ceiling, occluding its sculptured lead texture, and the place smelled of sweat and stale beer. Sean kicked his way through sawdust, eggshells, and cigar butts an inch deep on the plank floor and moved through the ranks of men, all facing a long painting of a reclining amply endowed, blond-haired nude, who stared down at them in regal, if cold, indifference.

Rosco Pugh had spared no expense on the bar, the back-bar, or his inventory—bottles four deep lined the mirrors, and six bunged barrels of whiskey rested there in sullen silence, awaiting the evening rush, three at each end.

Sean shouldered his way to the bar, acquiring the hard glances of a few of the linsey-woolsey–shirted, canvas-panted men as he did so. Other men concentrated on the play at the sparsely occupied green-felt–covered tables where faro, poker, and roulette were underway, or on the musician seated in a far corner who was busy with a stirring rendition of *Greensleeves* on a Prince mandolin and ignored the tall newcomer. But he moved between them unconcerned, standing a half head taller than most and at the moment driven by a pillar of white-hot heat that scorched his backbone and scalded his neck. He was damned tired of seeing "No Irish Need Apply," on help-wanted signs, and the lower his supply of silver got, the angrier he became. He didn't bother to remove the narrow-brimmed black hat he wore. He didn't figure on staying long.

But he did figure on leaving with a pocket full of coins.

The sign over the bar stated BAR WHISKEY $.25, A CHUNK OF SITKA ICE, ADD A DIME. Hell, it cost as much for ice as it did for beer.

The man behind the bar worked his way down to where Sean leaned, wiping beer foam and wet glass rings as he came. The wide garter that encircled his biceps over a starched white shirt had *Rosco's* embroidered in red on silk-trimmed black silk, and it was easy to read, for the man's thick arms could have accommodated Rosco Pugh's Saloon in half-inch letters with room to spare. He eyed Sean with indifference matching that of the oil painting over his head, sweat glistening from his receding hairline.

"Well?" he asked.

" 'Tis a deep subject, my friend," Sean answered, his feigned good humor belying the knot of anger in his gut, but the man either didn't get it or chose to ignore it. Neither of them smiled.

"Do you want something to drink or are you just holding up my bar?" The man placed both his hands on the bar, his fingers the size of corncobs, and hunkered forward, his unblinking blue eyes a challenge.

Sean sized him up, equaling the indifference he had received from both man and buxom oil painting. The barman was one of the few men in the place as tall as Sean, but his shoulders and chest were heavier. The barman appeared ten years older that Sean's own twenty years, and he suspected that the man was already going to fat: he'd find out soon enough, if the barkeep was Pugh.

"I'll be having a beer," Sean said, focusing his own dark eyes on the barman's lead-blue ones. *A bloody black-haired, blue-eyed Welshman son-of-a-whore, I'll wager,* Sean thought, and the heat in his neck began to creep around to splotch his throat.

"I got a half-dozen kinds of beer, friend, and I'm no mind reader."

"The cheapest," Sean said, knowing they all cost a dime a mug, and not taking his green eyes from the cold blue ones of the barman. "An' y'said 'your bar' . . . does that mean y'be Rosco Pugh his'sef?"

"That I am, friend. Lord of the manor," Rosco said proudly, as he tilted a mug under a spigot under the Ohio Brewery Dark and drew a white-capped glass of deep-brown ale.

"Then you'll be related to the man who has the sign in the window?"

"Not only related, but one and the same. Barman, and freighter of fine liquor, paints, and dyes, to the far reaches of the Sierras," Pugh said, extending his hand palm up. "That'll be a dime." He held the beer back until Sean dug into his worn, dusty canvas trousers and pulled out the necessary coin and dropped it on the bar, ignoring Pugh's wide waiting palm.

The barman snatched it up with a growl, slid the mug to Sean, then started to walk away.

"I imagin' with all y'many talents y'd be blacksmithin' for a colleen or two?" Sean asked, his eyes guileless. Rosco Pugh stopped short, turned, and stomped back. He obviously didn't like Sean's inference that he would stoop to act as a pimp, though most barmen did so, and even though "blacksmithing" was the politest way to refer to the practice.

His voice increased in volume as he approached. "Look, friend, there are ladies who make their living out of this bar, and that's their business, but I doubt if they'd be interested in entertaining the likes of you. Now you can finish your beer, then be on your way."

"Are ya a man who enjoys a ditty?" Sean asked, tipping his mug up and draining it while Rosco Pugh glared at him across the polished bar. Pugh's massive shoulders hunkered forward in an intimidating manner. Sean pulled one of the towels hanging under the bar and wiped the beer foam from his mouth.

"I've got no time for foolishness. Do you want another? . . . You can have one more if you've got the coin."

"Ah, a true businessman ya be, then." But rather than reach for a coin, Sean began to sing softly:

> I'm a dacint boy, just landed from the town of
>   Ballyfad,
> I want a situation: yis, I want it mighty bad.
> I saw a place advertised. It's the thing for me,
>   says I;
> But the dirty spalpeen ended with: No Irish
>   Need Apply.
> Whoo! says I; but that's an insult—though to get

104

the place I'll try.
So, I went to see the blaggar with: No Irish need
apply.

"That does it, mick," Rosco bellowed, but Sean went on, his
voice growing in volume.

Whoo! says I; but that's an insult—though to get
the place I'll try.
"So, I went to see the blaggar with: No Irish
need apply."

"Blackguard, is it?" Rosco reached across the bar and tried to
grab Sean, but he stepped back out of the barman's reach.

Sean ended his song with a bellowed chorus that quieted the
room and attracted the attention of every man in the place.

Sean's voice rang over the quiet. "I'd imagin' y'd be a bloody
Englishman . . . an' I'd wager a muckraking Welshman, with a
name like Pugh—or was it Puke—and with a heart black as
bloody coal and breath that stinks of kissin' the queen's broad
backside."

Rosco Pugh stood red faced, then spat onto the sawdust
covered floor behind the bar. "As the sign says, mick, 'no Irish
need apply.' Now you've had your song and you got no encores
coming, so get on down the road with you before I skin you
and use your hide for bar wipe."

By this time, all eyes had turned to them. Even the mandolin
player stopped his plinking.

"I don't suppose y'd be a bare-knuckle man?" Sean asked
loudly, again sizing Rosco Pugh up, only this time in an exag-
gerated manner.

"Just get the hell out of my place afore I have these men
heave you out into the mud."

"Then y'would be a Welshman, and a coward they all are,"

Sean said, his smile becoming a smirk.

"Throw him out, boys!" Pugh bellowed.

"Now wait, me lads." Sean extended his upraised hands, palms outward in supplication. "It's not y'boys who I'm casting dispersions upon, it's this ugly Welsh lout who shows his English ignorance with a sign like that one leering from his window. If he's half the man his unwed mother has claimed to every filthy miner in Wales"—he cut his eyes to Pugh—"as they rode her to a lather"—and grinned from ear to ear before he continued—"then he'll meet me in a bare-knuckle match right here in the center of this pigsty he calls a saloon . . . with gold coin to the winner!"

Rosco Pugh had had enough. Red faced and blowing spittle like a snapping cur, he didn't even bother to round the bar but rather clambered up and over it. Sean studied him as he came, glad the man didn't vault it easily.

"I've got a twenty-dollar gold piece," Sean lied at the top of his lungs, "that says I'll put him toes up on his own barroom floor before the half hour has passed."

"Done!" a drunken miner yelled from his seat at the faro table. He was joined by a number of others, who also called the bet as Rosco Pugh dropped from the bar and landed with a thump that indicated his heavy solid weight and began removing his studs and rolling up his sleeves.

His face glowed red, but he moved with a deliberation that Sean did not like. This was a man used to bare-knuckle brawls, with the shoulders and deep chest to back his play. Sean decided he would have to work this one like a mongoose toying with a cobra, before he landed him.

"Hand that iron on your hip to someone, mick, an' let's see if yer hands are half as good as yer liver lip," Pugh said, pulling his shirt off altogether, exposing arms, shoulders, and chest rippling with muscle.

No fat on this one, I'm sorry to note. Sean McKenna unstrapped his gun belt and flipped it to a nearby man, who laid it on a faro table, then Sean grinned with a confidence he didn't feel. "Let's get this over with. I've got more important business where a Welsh-whippin' Irishman *might* apply."

Rosco Pugh lowered his big head and charged like a bull.

Two doors down from Pugh's saloon, Ted Judah and Doc Strong walked from the door of Strong's Drug Store to stand under a suspended mortar and pestle—the only sign the drugstore needed. Both men smiled broadly. The night before, they, along with the packer they had employed, Jake McKenna, had returned from nearly two months in the high mountains doing preliminary survey work on Doc's trans-Sierra route. And the expert surveyor, Ted Judah, was convinced they had found the route he had been seeking so long. All day they had been reviewing their measurements and altitudes, then drawing an agreement between the two men, who would share equally in the venture. Only one small item remained: raising the capital. And since Ted Judah was still employed by the Sacramento Valley Railroad as its chief engineer, they would have to do the money raising on his off time.

But both were convinced that task would be easily accomplished.

Now, a celebration was in order to seal the bargain—and since Anna, Ted's wife, was in Sacramento, Ted would join in a drink.

"We ought to find Big Jake and invite him to join us," Doc suggested. "No one worked harder at accomplishing this survey." They strode down the boardwalk toward Rosco Pugh's Saloon.

"He said he was going to spend the day cleaning up the gear and shoeing his mule," Ted said. "He must be at MacGillicutty's Livery."

"Let's have one drink, then go find him. That'll give us an excuse to have another."

Just as they reached the batwing doors of the saloon with Doc in the lead, and as he shoved to enter the doors, they crashed open, knocking him sprawling into the road.

"What!" Ted jumped aside in surprise, but the man who stumbled out charged back in as quickly. Ted strode over to help Doc Strong to his feet and found Doc smiling.

"Looks like Rosco is at it again," Doc said. "Let's get in there and watch the blood, beer, and teeth fly."

They shoved through the doors and elbowed a space among the circled men. In the center of the room, Rosco Pugh and an equally tall man were stalking each other, both men bleeding from a variety of cuts and bruises. The crowd roared in encouragement and shouted wagers back and forth.

"Get 'im, Irish!"

"Knock him loop legged, Rosco!"

"What started this?" Doc asked a whiskered miner who was standing with clenched fists, feinting and ducking as the men battled. He answered without taking his eyes from the combatants.

"Irishman took offense at Rosco's help-wanted sign, 'No Irish Need Apply.' He's bet more'n a hundred dollars in gold that he can put ol' Rosco out."

"He seems to be holding his own," Doc said as Rosco Pugh closed and had his wild swing deftly blocked. The Irishman cracked him with two solid blows, snapping Pugh's head back and sending him reeling into the crowd. They as quickly pushed him back to the center of the ring of spectators.

Both men were panting heavily, but neither seemed close to quitting.

Again, Rosco charged and, even though he took another crashing right to the side of his head, managed to drive the

Irishman back into the crowd. Two of the men watching, obviously siding with the saloon owner, grabbed the Irishman's arms, pinning them to his sides. Rosco didn't miss the opportunity and smashed the man's face with a rain of powerful blows. Others in the crowd who had bet the other way fell on the two holding the Irishman's arms and jerked them away, almost coming to blows themselves.

Rosco Pugh backed off, convinced that the sandy-haired lout was finished as he sagged to his knees, but the Irishman shook his head, looked up and grinned at Pugh, and climbed to his feet. Blood poured from his nose, and one eye was puffed and nearly closed; Rosco bled from a split cheek and a smashed lip. Both men's knuckles were skinned and bleeding.

The Irishman spat a mouthful of blood, then raised his fists again.

"You'll be going down, y'ugly Welshman, sure as St. Patrick drove y'brothers, the slimy serpents, from me lovely Ireland."

The Irishman stalked forward, and Pugh sighed deeply, seeming to require a lot of effort to raise his fists to meet the new attack.

"Rosco!" one of the men in the crowd yelled to the barman, who cut his eyes just in time to see the brass knuckles the man had tossed fly in his direction. He caught them deftly and slipped them on his right hand.

"Come on, you Irish scum," he said, a look of triumph covering his bleeding face.

Sean McKenna circled the man, just as another fight broke out behind him. Four brawling men crashed into Sean's back, shoving him forward.

A crashing round-house brass-knuckled right missed Sean's face but smashed into his shoulder, careening him back against the wall. Sean's Colt had been knocked to the floor, and, instead of going after him, Rosco Pugh dove for it as the whole saloon erupted in a melee of fighting men.

I'm a dead man, Sean thought, knowing he could not close with the barman before he would get a shot off, then realized that just over his head was a peg holding a rope that rose at an angle to the ceiling. Suspended from it was a five-foot-round wrought-iron light fixture blazing with a dozen oil lamps—right over Rosco Pugh's head.

With death in his eyes, Rosco ratcheted back the hammer on the weapon. Sean swiped at the peg, knocking it flying and freeing the rope.

Rosco's mouth dropped open, and he just had time to glance up, when the wrought-iron fixture enveloped him. Glass chimneys smashed, as well as the heavier oil containers, and flames suddenly surrounded Rosco Pugh.

Men stopped in the midst of battling, and the place went suddenly dead still, then miners, hostlers, merchants, and drovers fought to find a route of escape as tendrils of fiery oil crept across the barroom floor in every direction.

Sean cut his eyes from front to back, then bolted to the rear behind two dozen escaping men, pausing only long enough to scoop a handful of gold coins from an abandoned faro table.

By the time he managed to squeeze out the rear door and run past the privies, the clapboard saloon was awash in flames.

"By the saints," Sean McKenna said when he finally stopped in the rear of a number of Dutch Flat business establishments to stare at the growing fire.

"It's him!" a man nearby yelled, and Sean realized it was he who had attracted their attention. Before he could run, a dozen men fell on him while others were more productively forming a bucket brigade.

They smashed him to the ground and pummeled him with fists and feet.

"Hang the bastard!" he heard a man shout, then consciousness faded as blow on blow rained on him.

Doc Strong and Ted Judah had backed out of the saloon almost as quickly as they had entered, running into their packer, Jake McKenna. The three of them were among those forming the bucket brigade from horse trough to saloon.

"What the hell happened?" the broad-shouldered, darker-haired McKenna shouted to Doc Strong as they passed buckets.

"Some wild-eyed countryman of yours picked a fight with Rosco Pugh, and in the melee the oil lamps smashed and lit the place like Hades."

"Who was he?" Jake asked.

"Didn't get his name . . . look at that!"

Down the street a half a block, a number of men had the tall sandy-haired Irishman on his feet, while another man looped a rope over the upper balcony rail of a two-story rooming house. On the balcony above, four women in gaudy lace covered gowns that proclaimed their dubious trade helped adjust the rope. A drover was busily tying a hangman's knot in the other end.

"That's the Irishman!" Doc yelled over the clamor.

Jake's eyes widened. "That's me bloody brother," he said, stopping in his tracks, staring in disbelief at the brother he had not seen in better than ten years.

Doc watched as Jake McKenna bolted down the dirt road with surprising agility for a man of his size. He smashed into the group of men holding Sean McKenna, still more unconscious than conscious, knocking them sprawling into the road. Sean sunk to his hands and knees.

Before the men could recover, Jake McKenna was panning his Remington revolver back and forth in a deadly challenge.

No one moved.

"Get to y'feet, Sean," Jake said quietly.

"Jake!" he managed, shaking his head to clear the cobwebs.

"Get to y'feet, now. We're getting out of here."

111

"He started that fire," a man said, struggling to regain his feet. "He's gonna hang."

"And y'gonna die right here in the road, friend," Jake said with deadly resolve, "if you put another hand on me brother or on that iron on y'hip."

The man took a step backward, his wide eyes glued to the big .44 in Jake McKenna's rawboned hand, and his hand carefully moved away from the pistol he wore.

Sean managed to climb to his feet, and he and Jake backed into an alleyway between the rooming house that had almost become Sean's gallows and a neighboring dry-goods store.

Doc Strong and Ted Judah watched them go. The men who had been so concerned with hanging Sean McKenna moved a step toward the alley, but the roar of a pistol and a plume of dust in front of them scattered them in every direction—save toward the alley.

Someone yelled for help, and the others in the road turned their attention to saving Horace's Tonsorial Palace, the closest Dutch Flat business establishment to Rosco Pugh's Saloon, forgetting, at least for the time being, Sean McKenna.

By the time the hanging party regrouped, Jake and Sean Mc-Kenna were long gone.

"I didn't know Jake had a brother," Doc said over the clamor of the line of men still hopelessly passing buckets.

"Told me he had two," Ted said, gasping for breath as he dipped and filled another bucket, then heaved it on, "one back East and one here in California . . . but he'd not seen them in years."

"Good thing he saw this one when he did. Those crazy louts would have hung him sure."

"Pass that bucket." Ted glanced at the building next to Pugh's and chastised his new partner to hurry, and they continued their work.

Jake McKenna, astride a big buckskin gelding, followed by a beaten and battered Sean McKenna uncomfortably astride Jake's wooden-pack-saddled mule, pounded out the rear door of MacGillicutty's Livery at a gallop, leaving Dutch Flat and its angry but busy residents behind.

When they finally slowed to a walk, well out of town on a wagon road lined with oaks, Jake reined back so Sean could trot alongside.

"Nice to see y'again, little brother," Jake said, a hint of sarcasm in his voice.

"Not as nice for ya as t'was for me, big brother. Ma would have never forgiven me if I got meself hung so far from home. What would she ha' told the vicar?"

"I left a good job back there," Jake groused.

"Not with Rosco Pugh, y'didn't," Sean said, a wide grin on his face. " 'No Irish need apply,' he said, so I applied me knuckles to his ugly mug. The last time I seen 'im he was slapping the flames on his trousers, wearing a light fixture for a 'oop skirt, an' cloggin' as fine a jig as y'd a' seen in all Kilkenny."

"Let's just hope the next time he sees you, that y're not dancing a jig at the end of a rope," Jake said, then reined up as he heard the pounding of hooves behind them.

"A bloody posse," Jake said, flashing his brother a hard look. "Every time I see ya, y're trouble." He gave spurs to the buckskin, reining off the road into the thick stand of oaks. Sean stayed close behind, not a bit interested in awaiting the approaching riders.

Sean laughed. "Who needs a damnable job anyways. I got us a pocket full a gold coin. All bloody bastard Pugh's got is a pile of ashes. Now all we gotta do is outrun a bunch of lazy louts who wouldn't take an honest job if it jumped up and slapped 'em in their ugly mugs."

Jake was not prone to smiling, but he did, then added, "I'll bet a month's wages that hell with freeze over before Pugh puts another 'No Irish Need Apply' sign in his window."

With the mule's rough gait, Sean had trouble getting it out but added, "The bastard's got no window."

GLORY HOLE

I'm hunkered down in river willows, the quiet Ruby River not ten paces from my hideout, while a column of Crow approach. At first, I worry they are on the prod for women or horses or whatever the savage goes on the prod for on a fair fall day with alders turning yellow, deer and elk in full antler glory, and antelope herding up to begin their rut. It will not be a good time to die when skeins of geese, ducks, and swans head south overhead and the morning air is refreshing and makes a man want to rejoice in living. Then again, I'm not sure it's ever a good time to die.

Just past my second score of years I have already acquired more than a bushel basket of sins for which to atone, and a fella would need a couple of score more years to have time to do so. And for just a moment I think I'm not going to get but another few minutes to do so as one of the dozen hounds running with the Crow turns my way, then stops short not a half-dozen paces and eyes me. He snorts as if he's nosed a pile of chili powder, then sneezes. I haven't soaked in a cold stream in two weeks so I can understand his reluctance to whiff any closer. Then the good Lord spares me as the pup loses interest and bounds away. And it seems I'll live another day.

That feeling is reinforced when the column of a dozen braves is trailed by a dozen paints and spotted Appaloosa horses led by ladies of the tribe and children, some of the women with boards and babes strapped to their backs, most with a youngster or two alongside, the horses burdened with travois loaded with teepees and everything they needed for their next encampment.

I'd have already tried to slip away, back to the river to float quietly downstream on one of the many busted-up chunks of cottonwood lining the bank, had the braves and the mounts I first spotted been painted for war. But they are not, and families following is the best of signs. And to do so would mean to distance myself from Snort and Grunt, my gelding and mule I've left ground staked in a tiny trickle-fed meadow a couple of hundred paces up above the river in a copse of lodgepole pine. It has become my habit to hide my stock far from where I grub in the mud and pan as they are more easily seen, and heard, than a body working alone, ofttimes in knee-deep water.

My sins are yet to overtake me.

But I am not about to push my luck, so I stay hunkered down giving the riders, walkers, and draggers time to wander a half mile downriver.

Six months ago, before the cottonwood began to leaf out, I'd given up a life of whiskey, cards, and dice, smoky saloons, and the occasional soiled dove for the healthy life of grubbing in the mud for gold. Rumors of gold in the trickles feeding the Yellowstone, the Gallatin, the Madison, and the Jefferson echoed through every bawdy house, gambling hall, army encampment, and anywhere else more than one pilgrim gathered. But after leaving St. Louis and riding a sidewheeler, the *Alabama,* on the Mighty Mo all the way to the mouth of the Yellowstone, disembarking with my fine sixteen-hand Morgan gelding and fifteen-hand coal-black Missouri mule and all the accoutrements, I figured, and had been advised, I'd need to find my God-given fortune in the ice-cold nooks and crannies of some Montana territory headwater.

But the hell of it is, I've been sorely disappointed on dozens of streams. My back aches like an Irish tater picker, my hands are blistered, I'm covered with welts from clinging brush and mosquitos doing their own mining, but them for blood. And they aren't the only savages about with a blood lust.

The color I'd collected wouldn't fill the bowl of the pipe I am now filling with Indian tobacco, which was all offered way back down the Yellowstone in the trading post at the mouth of the Tongue River. I'm happy to note, after springing the lid, my tinder box is doing its job, and I have enough spark to fire the tobacco—if you can call what the savage smokes tobacco. I was almost as disappointed by the lack of a few twists of real tobacco at the trading post as I was by the fact they'd been robbed of every mouthful of whiskey not a week before my arrival. It seems my growing loneliness will not be assuaged by the occasional snort—I'd promised to limit myself to a swallow a day—unless I come upon a generous pilgrim. Whiskey has long ago proven to bring out the worst in me. It awakens the thief and cheat. The very cousin of Beelzebub hides in the recesses of my bones and marrow, and I've sworn to let him rot there, never to awaken again. My stores are growing scarce, my enthusiasm wanes nearly as much as my flour and coffee, and I've about decided my past sins are far from redeemed by fresh air, snow-fed streams, and a diet supplemented by firm, fresh rainbow trout, rock-killed spruce grouse, the occasional snared snowshoe, and all the berries and watercress a fella can stand. I am pleased to discover I can live well without burning precious powder and peppering the hills with lead—and, more importantly, without alerting the savages to my presence with the roar of my .56-56 repeating Spencer. Two crockery quart jugs of Who Hit John had appeased my loneliness before I reached the Big Horn River but now are only a distant memory.

Just as well.

I go back to panning until the sun dips below the Tobacco Root range to the west, then return to my stock and make camp in the meadow where the thick lodgepole will provide not only cover from the eyes of the savage but plenty of easily gathered blowdown to fuel my supper fire.

For most of a week I work my way upstream, careful to find a crevasse or thick stand of trees to conceal the stock before breaking the pan out of Grunt's panniers and scooping a fistfull of sediment from behind a rock or atop hardpan beneath the mud or sand. That whole time I don't collect enough color to tip the scales of an assayer if I could find one nearer than five hundred miles. That is the bad; the good is the savage seems to have left the high country deciding it will be an early winter. I was told they can foretell the need of cords of wood by the length of the grasshoppers or the fuzz on some caterpillar, some knowledge well beyond my ken.

The nights are growing colder; the bugles of elk ring down from the timber above the river's alluvial-formed plains. If I don't find my glory hole soon, it will mean having to stop my quest for riches to build a sturdy enough shelter, stock firewood, and dry fish and jerk whatever critter I can kill to last the winter. I do have four beaver traps among my folderol, so all may not be lost when ice laughs at my attempts to grub the bottoms, should I master the art of trapping in order to capture and pelt-out the critters.

It is late on a cool afternoon more than a mile up a skittering crick, the sky as gray, flat, and still as one of my sainted mother's pewter platters, when my pan sparkles like the eyes of the angels. More gold in that single pan than I've collected since I led Grunt and Snort down the gangplanks of the sidewheeler *Alabama* at the trading post, the location of which was rumored to become an army fort, where the Yellowstone roils into the even wider Missouri. My mouth goes dry, and I quell the urge to dance a jig, yell, and praise the God I've been silently insulting for months.

Of late I've been lamenting the fact I didn't choose to stay aboard that belching floating bomb, *Alabama*, and continue to the end of the line, Fort Benton, and find employment skinning the pilgrims at a faro, poker, wheel of fortune, or dice game. With the flashing pan, I give it no more thought.

For a week I work from the first promising streaks of sunlight over the Madison Range to the east to the last sputtering red outlining the Tobacco Roots on the west. My poke is full, and I take time to cut a chunk from my buffalo robe to sew another. It's amazing the talents you glean from the cold-lonely when a thousand or more miles from the nearest mercantile.

Howsomever it's been ten days, and all color avoids me. It seems the Lord is again thumbing his nose at this poor pilgrim. But the fact is, I am no longer so poor. I figure I have two pounds in my pokes; thirty-two ounces at sixteen dollars the ounce is more than merely a good few days' work—in fact it's more than a year's pay for many. That said, I had hopes of rivaling him who built that Taj Mahal in far-away India.

But it seems it is not to be.

Just as the nights become cold enough to form ice along the banks of the stream, I am surprised to look up from my swishing pan to see two fellas, mounted, leading two mules each, and each mule with bulging panniers. They are perched not a hundred yards away atop a ledge. They sit quietly, eying me with some surprise, I imagine.

By this time, I've grubbed for nearly two weeks upstream from my glory hole with not enough shows to excite a two-bit a flop whore.

I give them a wave.

They wave back, spin their mounts, and disappear, I presume to work their way down to join me.

The angel perched on one of my shoulders quickly is shouted down by the demon on the other. I don't have much time.

Quicker than a flushed duck I hurry up the slope to where I'd hidden my pokes, grab one and my Spencer rifle. I know better than most that even a white man is not always to be trusted. I return and salt the hole I was working with a palm full of nuggets, at least two ounces, and pocket another ounce. Then I hurry back and hide the bearskin pouch again. I stand, rifle at easy rest against a thigh, and wait.

They rein up a hundred feet away, and I appreciate their caution. Both have rifles across their thighs and the pommels of their saddles as one waves and yells out, "Howdy the camp. Suit you we ride on in?"

And I yell back, "Suits me fine. You two are the first civil faces I've seen in more'n three hundred miles."

They ride on near, dismount, and, displaying a friendly nature, sheath both rifles. Both wear knifes that would cause Colonel Bowie some envy, but only one sports a sidearm, and it is secured in a flapped holster.

"Trappin' or grubbin' for color?" the taller of the two asks.

"Trying a little of both," I reply. "I have more of a camp up in the trees, and a haunch of deer I haven't jerked yet. I can offer that, but not much more. Could make us a stew, venison and wild onions, should you care to join me."

"You done any good with that pan?" the shorter one, with a chest like a beer barrel, asks.

"Don't guess I know y'all well enough to discuss business," I say, purposefully teasing a little.

"You short of sowbelly and hardtack?" the tall one inquires.

"And coffee and flour and damn nigh anything worth crossing a tongue."

Both of them laugh, and the tall one steps forward and extends a big paw. "I'm Clute Clemmings, recently . . . if two years past is recent . . . of New Orleans, and this here is my cousin twice removed Alvin Pasternac. How about we share a jug of whiskey, some bacon and beans, and some hardtack?"

Seems a fine time to lie. "I'm Lucky Louie Lanahan. Friends call me Lucky. Pleased to make your howdy."

They'd been soaking beans for two in a canteen, so I roast a pound of venison, chunk it into a pot of beans, and we share the jug as the mess boils a little softer.

They seem like solid sorts, and by the time we've stuffed ourselves we seem like fine friends, at least to them. Unfortunately, the dew of the corn has awakened the demons that dwell in my marrow.

I sense Clute is the older of the two as he does the most talking. He asks, "You turned up any color?"

"I ain't looking for any partners," I reply, remaining coy.

"We been in these mountains for two years and could use a little luck."

"Well, hell, you seem fine fellas, so this could be your lucky day. Ol' Lucky Louie here has been blessed with enough luck for all of us'n."

"The hell you say," Alvin says, his eyes beginning to widen.

"What I say is do y'all have anything to buy into my claim with? Fine smiles and a few pounds of supplies won't fill the bill."

It was Clute's turn to speak up. "We got lots of supplies, and you seem to be in need."

"Supplies don't buy that fine farm I got picked out back near Cairo, Illinois. What else you got?"

"Ol' pard," Clute said, his eyes narrowing, "we don't know what you got to sell."

So, I reach into my pocket and produce the handful of nuggets. "That there was two pans just before y'all swooped down on me from up on that yonder ledge."

"Bullshit," Alvin snaps.

So I merely shrug. "I'll bet if y'all wander up nearly any of these nearby streams you can color up a pan in no time."

"Two pans, eh?" Clute asks.

"Two pans, as God is my witness." I should have my fingers crossed, but that doesn't signal a truthful nature.

"Easy to say, hard to prove," Clute mumbles.

"And if I prove it, how much you got to buy in?"

"Give us a minute," Clute says and rises and pulls Alvin up, and they walk a few paces away, nearly out of firelight, and put their heads together for a few seconds, then return and plop down on the rocks they'd been occupying.

Clute clears his throat, then offers, "We'll buy your claim for two hundred dollars in gold pieces."

I laugh. "I wouldn't sell for ten times that," and I yawn and stretch. "Of course, I could use some partners. I'll sell you ten percent of the take for that two hundred, and that only 'cause I've taken a shine to y'all."

He puffs up a little, then mumbles, "My pa said never to be on the short end of a partnership."

I yawn again, then ask offhandedly as if not really interested, "I don't imagine y'all play cards or dice?"

"Gambling's a fool's errand," Clute says with a snort.

"I played some dice a time or two," Alvin says, and I could tell he was covering some confidence with the little ivories.

So, I rise and walk over to Grunt's pannier and dig out three pairs of dice. "I know a game so simple even a stupid Louisiana frog could learn it."

Clute takes a little umbrage at that, which is exactly what I meant to happen. His voice lowers an octave. "A fella could get his nose bent insultin' them he barely knows."

I ignore him. "Tell you what: I know this simple game called liar's dice. Learned it from a preacher man back in St. Louie just afore I rode out. You roll one die for who goes first, then you both roll but cover your dice so as the other fella can't see."

So I roll the dice behind a cupped hand so he can't see. "Like that . . . then him who won the first turn calls out a number, say 'two sixes,' and the other fella can better the number or call the first fella a liar."

Clute scratches his head. "So, what makes up a hand?"

"The fun of it is you combine the hands. Those three dice you can see, and those in the other fella's hand you can't see. If there are two sixes, combined, the fella called it wins. If not, he loses. Let's play a couple of hands so you get it."

So, I roll three dice behind my covered hand and have an ace, a three, and a six. He rolls and covers nicely, and I suggest, "We didn't roll for first, so you go."

He nods and with some hesitation says, "Two sixes!"

I laugh and say, "You liar."

"How many you got?" he challenges and shows his hand: a three, five, and six.

"You win," I say. "Let's go again. My call first this time."

He nods, and we both roll.

I have a three, four, and five, so I call out, "Four fives."

He contemplates a minute, then eyes me as he says, "Liar."

I have only one, and he has only one. "Damn," I say, building his confidence, "you're too good or too lucky."

"So, what do you want to play for?" Alvin asks.

"Let me cogitate on that," I say, seeming in deep thought, then offer, "I'll tell you what: I'll make y'all full partners, one third for each of us, for four hundred dollars should you win. Should I win, y'all take one third for that same four hundred dollars. But either way, you throw in all the supplies you brung along."

Clute stands and shakes his head. "I ain't buyin' no pig in a poke, win or lose."

"Then," I say, looking innocent, "I'll let you decide tomorrow, after the sun is over the yardarm, and we can see to pan.

Tomorrow, you can decide to buy in or not, but only after I pan one pan full. I ain't givin' you a month to decide. If I win you buy in for half for the both of you for four hundred, after you decide. But if you decide *no,* I get half your supplies."

"I'm confused," Alvin says.

"I'm not," Clute says. "We play, and if he wins, we get the option to buy half for four hundred after he pans one pan full."

"So, what if we win?" Alvin asks.

"Then you can have two-thirds for that same four hundred, if you decide to buy in."

"Sweet Jesus, man," Clute replies, "It doesn't look like we can lose. We can only win one way or the other."

"Well, like I said, I want me some partners. It's lonely as hell here, and y'all got enough grub to last us the winter."

"Let's play," Alvin snaps.

"To show you fellas how fair I am, I'll let you go first." Knowing human nature as I do, he does as I suspect he will.

"No way. You go first."

"If you insist," I say.

"I'll do this," Clute says and grabs up the dice.

We roll, and, not being able to help myself, with both hands covering the dice, I reach down with a hidden thumb and do as I've done hundreds of times before. Unseen by either of them I manipulate the dice, turning two of them with a thumb so I have three sixes.

"You first," he says, grinning with only half his mouth as if he knows something I don't.

"Wait, wait," I say, "let me think." And I hesitate a while, then say, "Three sixes."

He smiles and exposes his dice—an ace, deuce, and a five.

"Ha," he says, "we ain't got a six."

"No problem," I say, "I got all three."

He eyes me with some suspicion, then shrugs. "So tomorrow

it's either half for us or nothing."

"Yeah, but I ain't panning unless I know you got the four hundred."

"We got it," Alvin snaps.

"Then show it," I say.

And he goes to the panniers, and I pay even closer attention to where he digs up the pouch. He turns his back to me and counts. Obviously, they have more than four hundred in the pouch. He finishes and walks back and lets one palm full of twenty-dollar gold pieces fall into the other.

I hold both hands out to my sides and shrug as I assure them, "Good enough. Sorry I doubted y'all."

I sleep soundly even with strangers in camp and awake with a smile, figuring I'd found my glory hole even if only filled with suckers, but suckers with full pokes.

We eat our fill of bacon and hard tack as the sun's rays promise a beautiful warm fall day and creep across the river, shadows moving away from us.

"What are we waiting on?" Clute asks as I down the last of the first coffee I've tasted in weeks.

"Nothing, I guess," I say and stand and stretch, then walk down to the river and gather up my pan, which I'd left exactly one generous pace downriver from the hole I've generously salted. "What do you think," I ask, "here or here?"

Both of them shrug. I skim the surface of the mud below, knowing the nuggets I'd dropped have had little time to work their way down an inch much less to bedrock, and make sure I can feel plenty of "pebbles" in the mess, then bring the pan to the surface and begin to slough off the mud and sand as I rock and swirl the tin pan. As I do, a half-dozen or more nuggets begin to reveal, and I can feel the breath of those staring over my shoulder and hear their breathing pick up the pace.

"Enough," Clute says. "Let me hold a few and test their weight."

I lay the pan down, pick up a few of the larger nuggets, and hand them to him.

He grins like a schoolboy who's just had his first kiss from the prettiest girl in class. "You have a deal, partner."

"Tell you what," I say, "you two let me do the cooking, and you do most of the grubbing, and, as the God-fearing Christian I am, I'll agree to that two-thirds. But we've got to have us a party in celebration for the rest of the day and drink us another jug, and not start the work 'til the morrow. Agreed?"

They laugh and do a little jig. And both say, talking over each other with their excitement, "A party it is. Hot damn. Rich fellas should have a party once in a while."

And we do have us a good ol' shindig. Eating and drinking and singing "Oh Susanna" and "Comin' Round the Mountain" until we're all hoarse throated and seeing double.

At least they are seeing double. I've paced myself.

Not long after they both snore away, I gather up all the gold in camp. All that I've panned and those coins in their pouches. I quickly split the load between one of their mules and Grunt and pack up and slip out of camp by moonlight.

They will have a rude awakening.

I have always wanted to see San Francisco, but know I have to ride east in order to find a way west, and the way west in style I can now afford. They had over nine hundred dollars in their poke; I had two pounds of dust and nuggets at sixteen dollars the ounce, another five hundred dollars plus change.

I'm richer than a sultan.

It takes me most of a month, the weather getting colder, thin break-through ice on the streams, to get back to the Yellowstone. Then another two weeks to enlist the aid of a couple of trappers who let me buy passage on their small flat-bottom boat down to the Missouri. I catch the last trip of the season on a boat I know well, the *Alabama,* and arrive in St. Louis without incident.

I decided to wait out the winter in St. Louis. The trip down to New Orleans, then to the Isthmus, then across, and a fine berth on a full rigged ship to the Sandwich Islands, then back to San Francisco will be much easier in the springtime.

The hell of it is, I didn't fulfill my alias as "Lucky Louie" while I lay over in the city. Seems I learned some expensive lessons on the poker table, even though I awake the devil in my bones by seeing the bottom of far too many bottles of fine Black Widow whiskey. The fact is, a large fella, some say a river man used to loading bales of cotton, takes umbrage at an ace he said found its way into my waistcoat pocket and breaks my arm with an easy twist. Snaps it just below the elbow as I reach for a hide-out gun on my ankle.

Unable to work, I soon deplete the rest of my funds.

By the spring I have to move out of the luxury St. Charles Hotel and take a shared room in the rear of the Pride of Paris, a saloon and bawdy house where I've taken a job dealing faro, mostly one handed.

No matter my circumstance, I figure I've had a good run, living a year in a fine hotel with the company of a dozen different soiled doves from time to time. That while those fools Clute and Alvin muck a frozen stream and dodge arrows and tomahawks. I've been lucky, even if now broke . . . luckier than those two fools I left to freeze through the winter near a phony glory hole I'd worked to nothing but mud.

It's summer, and to say I'm down in the mouth is a bit like saying the mighty Mo at my feet is wide, as I sit near the river and pick up a *Leslie's Weekly* someone has left on the bench. I'm trying to distract my thinking, as the sawbones has just informed me I should have been more selective about those soiled doves I hosted to Champagne and oysters in my St. Charles suite. It seems I've acquired the pox, and there's no cure.

The names on the front page, in a small article near the bottom, are familiar to me.

The article reads, "Clemmings and Pasternac discovery in Montana Territory, a true glory hole, yields sixteen million in less than a year of operation."

My teeth clamp so hard I'm not sure my jaw will ever come unstuck. I wonder if Clute and Alvin would consider another game of liar's dice? Of course, I won't live long enough to use my talented thumb on the suckers.

Glory hole? Looks as if mine will soon be in the paupers' section of the St. Louis cemetery.

EYE FOR EYE

CHAPTER ONE

The Big Horn Mountains, Montana, Spring 1876

Six dusty, trail-worn riders reined up, staying in the cover of a stand of lodgepole pine, two hundred yards from the log ranch house, barn, and corrals. Even at that distance and with lots of cover between them, the ranch dog knew their presence and was barking.

One man rode on, at a slow walk so as not to appear to have any malice in his heart.

A single rider . . . just wanting to water his horse after a long ride.

When Ranger, Quint's cow dog, started raising all Billy Joe hell, Consuela walked over and pulled a lace curtain aside, eyeing the yard from the window. Ranger hated crows and often went a little crazy when one landed in the yard—particularly if it was near his bowl. She figured that was what was troubling him and smiled, then returned to work.

Dressed in an ankle-length elk-skin dress and buffalo-skin moccasins, gifts from Two Hatchets, Consuela Reagan was carefully folding beaten egg whites into the batter for a cake that would bake up light as smoke. Her forehead wore a band of beads on soft elk skin, also a gift from the Sioux. Her long hair, black and shiny as a raven's wing, hung to the middle of her back and was pulled back and tied with a thong of woven rawhide to keep it out of her cooking. Her face wore a smile and had for the last two months, since she'd missed her monthly.

A gift of God—a child in her belly.

Tomorrow was their fifth anniversary, and she wanted something special for Quint, and he loved her cakes.

Quint had taken her away from Colorado and its horrible memories of the death of her father and the loss of a rancho that had been in their family for six generations.

But that was all behind her.

Now, Montana was a new life and Quiet Waters a new ranch and new opportunity, rich with deep grass and sweet water . . . all overlooking the wide Yellowstone River.

And she was with child, again, after losing the first one. Three months along, she figured.

God would finally bring them a child—the beginning, she hoped, of a large family. God willing this child would make it full term.

She paused a moment from beating the cake batter and listened. The clomping of hooves? Quint couldn't be home so early.

Walking over to the basin she washed her hands, then moved to the door and reached for the handle, just as there was a knock.

She opened the door to see a tall man with sharp features in a duster and floppy-brimmed hat, who politely stepped back from the door. He snatched the hat off his head before she could speak, holding it in both hands at his belt line.

"Ma'am, just passing through and thought you might have a little work for a hungry stranger?"

His voice was low and reassuring.

The man was unshaven and looked like it had been a week since he'd stropped a razor. His beard was gray, and he had a gray—almost white—stripe in the center of his dark head of hair from forehead to crown.

She gave him a tight smile. "You'd have to talk to my husband about that. But if you want to take a seat there on the porch, I'll fetch you something to eat."

"Why, ma'am, that's kind of you. You sure I can't carry some wood in or some such?"

She was running low. "Wood's in the shed on the far side of the house. I'll get something . . ."

As she moved back to the pie safe where she had some leftovers from last night's supper, she wondered how wise she'd been . . . now he'd come inside.

She filled a pie tin with cold elk stew and three tortillas and was pouring a cup of coffee when her door opened and he walked in, his arms heaped with stove wood.

He left the door wide, not the act of a man up to no good.

As he stacked the wood in the bin next to the Buck stove, he asked, "Can I speak with the man of the house?"

"He's out in the fields," she replied, which was a small lie, as he was working, in town, four miles upriver.

"He ain't here," the man said, loud enough that it could be heard across the farmyard.

Her mouth went dry. She cut her eyes to the door, and the shotgun on an antelope horn rack over the doorway.

The crooked smile he gave her sent a chill down her back. Her mouth went dry while her spine turned to ice.

He chuckled, then spat out, "You'll never make it, squaw woman."

"I'm Mexican," she said and broke for the door and the shotgun.

But he was right. He caught her by the wrist as another huge man filled the doorway.

The one with the stripe in his hair dragged her toward the only other room in the house and the double bed there. Screaming, her knees going to mush, she raked the side of his face with her free hand . . . her nails drawing blood and a vehement wail.

He spun and slapped her hard, then slapped her again and again until her legs folded under her, and, even with her ears ringing and half unconscious, she heard the laughter of more than one man who'd entered the house.

Then another man grabbed her arms, jerking her up, painfully wrenching them together behind her back until her elbows almost touched. Her eyes flared, and she screamed little more than a squeak as her mouth and throat had gone dry as a bone yard, as the first man tried to tear the buckskin dress apart to expose her breasts . . . then jerked a knife from the scabbard at his belt and split it and the chemise she wore beneath down to the waist. Her breasts spilled out, and he glared, then laughed hungrily.

"By God, she's brown as a bean, but she's all woman," he yelled, and others laughed.

All she could think of was the baby. No matter what happened, she must protect her unborn.

CHAPTER TWO

The Ragged Rock Ranch, the Triple R

Bradford Braddick, his hands folded behind his back, stood looking out his tall windows over the two hundred thousand acres of rolling grassland he owned or controlled and the many thousand head of cattle.

He was quiet for a long while, his foreman across the room leaning on the burl wood bar, sipping three fingers of Who Hit John. Finally, the big barrel-shaped man turned from contemplating the situation and, still angry, glared at his foreman. "God damn the flies, Spike, how the hell could you let this happen?"

"I told you, Brad, it was Oliver done the dirty deed. The other boys was just shaming the woman . . . she looked like a breed to me . . . but she kicked Terror right in the personals, and he grabbed her by the head of hair, jerked her up off'n that bed, and banged her head up against the log wall a half-dozen times afore we could get to him. You know how crazy the som'bitch can get. We tied her down on the bed so she wouldn't kick no more. Hell, when we left she was still breathing."

"Damned fool," Braddick murmured. "Damn, damn, damn fool. If he wasn't so good with a gun, I'd ride him out tarred and feathered. Are you sure y'all left nothing there to tie anyone back to the Triple R?"

"We left nothin' but tracks. Of course, they knew we was in that part of the country."

"Now, how the hell would they know that?"

"You don't think the boys would be that close to town and some pleasure ladies and not go in to who'ra the place, do you?"

Spike could see his boss's jaw knot, and he was beginning to get red in the face. "You went on into Big Horn. Hell, why didn't you visit the sheriff's office and tell him a half-dozen Triple R riders just poked his chile pepper wife?"

"Only five. Young Tony didn't poke her. Fact is he wouldn't even go inside. He still ain't talked to any of us." Spike guffawed, but the look he got from his boss sobered him.

"And for good reason. I'd hate to see him get his neck stretched for what you no goods did to that woman."

"You said rough her up."

"Rough her up and make her want to run for Mexico ain't beating her brains out, you damn dumb knot head."

Spike just stood, looking sheepish.

"Get the hell out. If that Reagan don't ride in here with a hundred men, I'll be damn surprised. He's a pilgrim, but the damn fool don't have an inch of back up in him. You brought a trainload of trouble to us, Spike. We'll have a hell of a time buying that place now."

"Wasn't me sent a bunch of owlhoots to trouble some woman."

Braddick moved forward in three swift steps and drove a corncob-sized finger into Spike's chest. "Look here, you been riding with me for damn nigh twenty years, but that won't keep me from riding you out of here astraddle a rail. You watch your mouth, and what others might be privy to." Braddick cut his eyes to the kitchen to make sure the help wasn't snooping.

Spike mumbled, " 'Sides, ain't no hundred men in Big Horn. And if'n he comes here with less, you'll buy the place from the new Big Horn sheriff who'll be auctioning it off for taxes . . . 'cause dead men don't pay no taxes."

"Get out, fool."

"Yes, sir." He spun on his booted heel and headed for the kitchen to leave via the back door.

"Hong, get in here," Braddick yelled, and in seconds his Chinese cook appeared in the doorway, wiping his hands with a towel.

Braddick continued, "How you fixed for supplies?"

"Have a keg of flour, have half keg of sugar. Twenty pounds Arbuckle's. Five pounds or more salt. Got a dozen pork bellies and two dozen hams in smokehouse. Got forty pounds of dried apples, two hundred pounds spuds and onions, and a sack of turnips in cellar. In good shape for a while."

"I want you to take the buckboard and your nephew and go to Big Horn and stock up."

"Mister, we got plenty."

"Who's the boss here, Hong?"

"When go?"

"Leave early in the morning. Go by Mrs. McLaughton's and

see what they might need, and see if'n she's ready to come back to the home place."

"You bossman." He started to turn, his long black braided queue swinging as he did so.

"Hong, I want you to talk to your people. What's that fella at the laundry?"

"Ling."

"You talk to Ling and any other Chinaman around Big Horn and see what the story is on Sheriff Quinton Reagan. I heard his wife died, and they think Triple R had something to do with it. Assure your people we didn't, and the word will get 'round."

"Closer I go Lewistown."

"God dammit, who's the bossman here?"

"Go Big Horn, go Mrs. McLaughton's, get supplies, talk Ling and other Celestials."

Hong nodded vigorously, his pigtail bouncing. He didn't bother to mention that he'd heard everything that went on at the Triple R, and probably knew more about what happened at the Reagan place than the boss did . . . but he also knew from long experience it didn't pay to know too much, or to let the round eyes know you knew anything.

He was almost out of the big living room when Braddick called after him. "And bring me a cigar and a touch of brandy."

"Yes, boss."

CHAPTER THREE

Sunday, six days later, Big Horn, Montana
"How're you doing, Reagan?"

"Ian, are you asking as my pastor or as my friend?" Quint Reagan replied with a sad smile, buckling on the gun belt he'd removed to enter McLean's little church. The other parishioners were moving around them and on down the wooden stairs. One or two of the men extended rough farm- and ranch-callused hands to shake with McLean and offered their congratulations on his sermon. A couple of them patted Reagan's broad shoulder but said nothing, as they knew there was little left to say.

They'd buried Consuela on Wednesday, out at the ranch. Most of the town had attended. Even the dozen Chinese all dressed in white as was their funeral custom. Quint had a yearling steer butchered and deep pitted, the women brought pots of other dishes, but Quint didn't eat and hadn't since he'd returned home and found Consuela.

He'd drunk some since, but whiskey offered little nourishmen, and didn't console him.

Reagan had to smile, knowing his old friend, Ian McLean, had aimed the do-unto-others sermon to strike him heart center. But it would take far more than words, no matter how well meaning, to detract him.

McLean, preoccupied with his friend, ignored the next man trying to shake with him. Turning to Reagan, he offered a tight smile. "Why don't you head back out to Quiet Waters and visit Consuela one more time, and maybe she . . . and that beautiful place . . . will convince you—"

"She's not talking from the grave, Ian. God willin', by now, her soul is at His right hand."

"God willin'." McLean quickly shook with the blacksmith—a big man, hard to ignore—then reached out and grabbed Reagan's shoulder as he started to move away.

"I'll go out with you, and we can pray at her graveside. Maybe you'll find some peace."

Reagan gave him a last sad smile. "Ian, I'm setting prayer on the fencepost for a while. Where I'm going, and what I plan to do, even the good Lord doesn't want to bear witness."

Ian sighed deeply. "Turn the other cheek, Quinton."

Reagan smiled. No one had called him by his full first name for a long, long time; only Consuela, when he angered her for one reason or another, and he hadn't done that often and never purposefully.

"I'll say goodbye to Consuela for you. I'm stopping back at the ranch to pick up Ranger and Kit and cleanse that place . . . so I'll say my goodbyes alone. I've sold the herd and given Mayor Riddick my power of attorney to sell the place to anyone other than the Triple R . . . so there's nothing holding me here. He's to give you the proceeds if I'm not around. You take ten percent for yourself or as a tithe, your choice. If you hear of my demise, you use the rest to build a church and school. Otherwise, I'll get word to you where to send a draft for the balance. And that location is for you and only you to know. Agreed?"

"As you wish. You've been a good friend to this town and this church."

Quint paused for a long moment, seeming far away, then eyed Ian and spoke with conviction. "An eye for an eye, Ian. That's my Biblical mantra until I finish this."

"Consider turning the other cheek, Quint. If for no other reason, Braddick has a hundred men, and you'll never get close."

"Then I'll join Consuela. I don't want 'em all, just the six that rode into town and the scum-suckin' man who sent them. I'm gonna roll a lucky seven. The six were under orders . . . they didn't stop by Quiet Waters just to wet their whistle. Braddick's long wanted the place, due to the year-round water, a place to winter those high-brow bulls of his."

Quint stretched and yawned, and Ian figured he hadn't been getting much sleep.

Then Quint continued and confirmed his suspicion. "Ian, I've got to finish this. Then I can sleep, and Consuela can rest in peace."

"Then keep the badge on and bring them in for trial."

"Not this time, Ian. I won't take the chance they'd get set free. Braddick has too much power and too much money."

"Revenge won't take you to the right hand of God, my friend."

"Then I'll be giving old Beelzebub my own brand of hell for the rest of eternity . . . if God doesn't believe in right."

Ian smiled as he walked with Reagan toward the big buckskin and stood back as he sucked up the latigo, gathered up the reins from the hitch rail, then mounted.

Ian stopped and stared, then shook his head sadly. "A Smith and Wesson Russian on your side, two Peacemaker Colts in saddle holsters, a double-barrel coach gun in the bedroll behind the cantle, and a Winchester in the saddle scabbard . . . you are bloody hell on the hoof, my friend."

"I hope you're right, Ian, for that's what I intend to be. Fact is, I plan to send a half-dozen Ragged Rock Ridge, Triple R riders to hell, along with that tub of guts who's their boss. That coach gun's loaded with cut-up square nails, and I plan to fill old puss gut's belly with them and hope he don't die too fast." He bent forward and offered a wide work-toughened hand to his pastor and friend. "Will you wish me luck?"

"Can't wish you success in this mission, Quint, but I can pray that you come home safe."

"Thanks to them that violated it, I don't have a home," Reagan said, removing the star from his vest and flipping it to Ian. "Return that to Mayor Riddick and the town council for me. I don't want folks thinking I'm on county business. If I light somewhere after all this is over, I'll drop you a line or a telegram as John Smith, and the name of a bank where you can send the draft."

Ian nodded but was still trying. "Quint, you're no gunfighter. I don't believe you've skinned that six-shooter the whole time you've been sheriff."

Quint had to laugh quietly. "Ian, I spent four years wearing the blue, sleeping with a Sharps. I haven't talked about it much as I take no pride in it. It was war. I did my duty. These six won't be the first to taste lead from my attentions. Stay well, my friend."

Ian sighed deeply, then said in a low voice, "Go with God."

"Not this time, but I'll try to find my way back to him if I live."

Ian merely nodded as Reagan reined away, then gigged the big buckskin into a lope, but only for a block, as he saw the storekeeper unlocking his door. He reined up and Gunter Albreit glanced up.

"I'm not open for business, Sheriff. Just gonna take the quiet time to straighten some shelves."

"Not sheriff any longer, Gunter," Reagan said, dismounting. "And I'm riding out, so this is your last chance to get any of my money. I got a tab here, and if you want it paid now, you'll sell me a few things as well."

"You need some supplies for your trip?"

"Just a few. Won't take long."

"Then come on in. Sorry about Consuela," he mumbled, and Quint merely smiled tightly and nodded.

Reagan had given a long last look at his friend the pastor, and it had given him an idea. He bought five pounds of jerked beef, a tin of salt, three pounds of Arbuckle's coffee, a five-pound slab of bacon, five pounds of dry beans, five pounds of flour, four pint jugs of Black Widow Whiskey, some lead and powder for his reloading, two boxes of 12-gauge double-aught bucks, and a half-dozen sheathed knives . . . for he had to ride through Indian country and needed some trade goods and gifts.

The last thing he added was a white celluloid collar, one of only two Gunter had in stock. He smiled. He'd never owned a collar although all his shirts were collarless, including the two he had packed in his saddlebags. It wasn't as if he were stepping up his wardrobe, but when you wore one reversed, people would presume you were a man of peace, a man of God . . . a preacher man. And he figured he might gain a little advantage from that subterfuge. He had to smile at the thought.

He paid his bill and his tab, bid the storekeeper farewell, and walked out. Before he mounted, he untied one of two canteens he carried on either side of the saddle, hanging below the bedroll and shotgun. With some care he untied the cloth sack the beans came in and poured the canteen a quarter full, two good handfuls, then brushed away the moss and refilled it with water from the trough in front of the general store. They'd be good and soaked and fit to cook by the time he made camp at nightfall somewhere near the Ragged Rock Ridge ranch property line over across the Yellowstone. The ranch headquarters were a couple of hard days' ride to the northwest on the edge of Judith Basin.

From then on, he'd be on the hunt. But first he had to stop by Quiet Waters—four miles down the river, east of the little town of Big Horn—to take care of three years' hard work and say goodbye to his wife.

The north border of Quint's spread lay from near the banks of the Yellowstone south a half mile and was small by Montana standards. Although it didn't border the river, it was well watered from south to north by Dirty Andy Creek, which flowed, in spots, year round, due to a couple of hot springs without a whisper of sulfur. His spread was small, but many thousands of acres of free graze were situated on the buttes to the south and east. So a fellow could raise as many cows as he could keep winter from killing or the Indians from stealing . . . or Braddick from rounding up and using a running iron to change the brand.

One of the mistakes old man Rockingham had made was

establishing the Quiet Waters brand as a simple wavy line with two humps, and the Ragged Rock Ridge brand had long been a wavy line with three humps and three verticals representing pine trees. Too damn easy for a man to alter with a running iron and even a modicum of art—or rustling—talent.

CHAPTER FOUR

Quiet Waters was a three hundred-twenty-acre homestead he'd bought from the Rockinghams at the foot of the Big Horn Mountains. They were an older couple who'd decided they just couldn't stand the pressure from the huge Ragged Rock Ridge spread—bad neighbors—to the north and renegade Indians to the south.

The Yellowstone ran lined with cottonwoods full of whitetail deer, wide and quiet, as it passed near the spread, thus the name.

Quint and Consuela made an offer on the place the first time they took a buggy there from Big Horn, where Quint had taken a job training horses for the hostler and livery.

Quint had fallen in love with a beautiful black-eyed Mexican girl in Southern Colorado, not long after the War Between the States. Consuela had lived near Pueblo, almost on the border with New Mexico, since the blessed day she was born. Her family had been there more generations than they could remember. Their spread was the result of a Spanish land grant, but before Quint had come along, her father had lost it all due to the chicanery of some Denver lawyers and was too old, and too frail, to fight back.

He'd passed just after Quint met Consuela—in fact, Quint had dug his grave.

The only job for a now poor, young, single, beautiful Mexican girl was in the city. And that job had no future but to die of the pox. As Consuela had always loved the high mountains and had travelled deep into the Rockies many times as cook for her father's cow camps, she had no hesitation when Quint asked her to marry and go north with him to find a place to ranch. North, along the Rockies, until they found a place to start a new spread. He sincerely hoped it was because she loved him as he did her, not because she was fighting shy of the brothel, but she came to prove it over the next year and beyond.

They'd worked for three different spreads in Colorado, Wyoming, and finally near Bozeman, where Consuela got pregnant. That, and the fact the Sioux and other tribes were on the run, kept them in one place for almost a year. When she lost the baby, and when General Miles and his foot soldiers walked Sitting Bull and Crazy Horse and their people down on the Tongue River, and shortly thereafter rounded most of them up and drove them to the reservation, Quint and Consuela headed out with a little savings to find a place to settle.

Quiet Waters had been that place.

There were still a few bands of renegade Indians running the hills, but Quint had been ready to share an occasional beef with the Sioux, the Crow, the Cheyenne, and the Assiniboine, and they'd gotten on fine. They only asked for help when the hunting was bad and their children starving, and he always complied. And never to his knowledge did they steal from him. In fact, they'd even repaid him with a haunch of buffalo and half an elk on different occasions. Two Hatchets, who Quint figured was a war chief of one of the Sioux bands, often stopped and shared a meal with Quint and Consuela, more than once with a mule deer backstrap to throw into the pot.

After a hard winter and the loss of half their herd, Quint took the job of sheriff in the little town of Big Horn. Work on the ranch had lessened, and, to his pleasant surprise, Consuela had gotten pregnant again. And was three months pregnant when she was killed while he was in town doing his job.

Six riders, proven by the tracks, had ridden into the ranch. When Quint returned home that night, he found her in their little bedroom, tied spread-eagle hands and ankles to bedposts. Naked, she must have fought before being subdued, as she was bruised, and her lip and a cheekbone were cut. But it was a blow to the head that caved her skull and killed her.

And there was a note, tacked to the bedroom door.

Squaw man, this will learn you.

The dumb bastards thought she was an Indian, probably thanks to an elk-skin dress Two Hatchets' woman had given her after she'd fed their family . . . not that Quint wouldn't have married one if he'd fallen in love with her as he had with Consuela.

What angered him even more was the fact the men had rode on into Big Horn after their heinous act, and he'd wondered why six drunken Triple R riders had laughed and cackled every time they'd passed him in the street, or when he came into the Wolverine Saloon. They'd put their heads together and occasionally cut their eyes at him and chuckled. Had he only known . . . There was a hole in his soul that would only be filled by the hard death of seven men.

He'd stayed in town later than usual, thinking the group of cowhands might cause trouble . . . but, in retrospect, he guessed they'd had their fill.

He'd stayed in town late, while Consuela lay dying. That left a putrid taste in his mouth that he figured he'd never, never, never get shed of.

God, if he'd only known.

What he did know was what they looked like and had gleaned names from the bartender who'd seen them before and even given some of them credit.

They were long gone when anger overtook his grief, and he galloped back to town, but he knew who they were, what they looked like, and what to carve on their gravestones . . . unless he let the crows and the coyotes have at them, which was more likely.

Spike Howard, tall and cadaverous with a prominent Adam's apple, the ramrod of the Ragged Rock Ridge, was the leader of the pack. Torrance Oliver, nickname Terror, with a scar from the bottom of his left ear to the puckered corner of his mouth was another; as were Antonio Balducci, nickname Baldy, who had a full head of curly black hair; Skunk Tobias, who'd gone gray in a two-inch-wide stripe from front to back of his full head of black hair; Charley Tall Horse, a half-black, half-Blackfoot Indian with an arched nose that would shame a Frenchman; and Shamus O'Shawnnaessy, a redheaded Irishman with a small mouth and tiny ears that made his head look oversized.

They—and Braddick—were in Quint's book, etched in his mind, their names burned there, seared deep into the gray matter. They were a festering wound that would only be healed by sending them, each and every one, to hades.

Quint dwelled on all these memories as he rode into the yard between the house and the log barn he'd doubled in size since they bought the place.

Consuela was buried up on a little rise that she favored, where one could sit on a fallen log and see up and down the Yellowstone for over four or five miles each way.

Ranger met him, barking and leaping up and down. He'd been told the dog was an Australian Shepherd, maybe part dingo dog, but all he knew for sure was that he was a hell of a cow dog, afraid of nothing, and smarter than some men he knew. He tied the buckskin to a rail and headed into the house for a last look but saw nothing that he'd take with him. He'd already given most of their belongings to the church. His mouth tasted of copper, not fear, as he eyed the framed sampler she'd hung on the wall: Welcome to Our Happy Home! God Bless All Who Enter.

The wool it was woven into seemed to scratch and burn the back of his throat and make his eyes water, and he had to wipe his nose on his sleeve.

He'd never seen Consuela turn someone away from their door, even if they didn't have enough.

He collected himself, then left the house with a purposeful stride, fetched Kit Carson—a small but very tough dun-colored mule—from his barn stall, and brushed him down and saddled him with a packsaddle. Hanging panniers off the saddle, he filled them with his grub and a few items he might need on the trail: a couple of spare horseshoes, some nails, some rope, and a couple of canvas pack covers. As an afterthought, he grabbed a pair of wolf traps off the rack on the wall and dropped them on either side of the packs.

Kit wasn't a big mule, just as his namesake hadn't been a big man, but he was tough as a grizzly bear and twice as willing to take on whatever got in his way. So he was well named.

Quint loved that dog and the mule, and maybe loved them even more so now that Consuela wasn't around to love.

When he was ready, he moved off a hundred feet from the house and barn and tied the buckskin and the mule to an elm, then returned.

The house was full of lots of river willow bentwood furniture he'd made with his own hands. Most of Consuela's things he'd already taken into town and given to Ian at the church in case he found some lady folks in need.

He took a deep breath, and a slow look around, then grabbed a jug of coal oil from under the kitchen sink and poured it from the kitchen all the way across the main room and into the bedroom. Emptying the jug into the center of the bed where Consuela had been so violated, he threw it aside and used a thumbnail to light up a Lucifer. He dropped it onto the oil-soaked goose-down comforter, then turned and walked out, across the yard, and into the barn.

Kicking some meadow grass hay into a loose pile, he thumb-nailed another Lucifer and tried to get it going, but it wouldn't light. A lantern hung on a nearby wall, and he retrieved it and shook it as he returned to the hay. Yes, there was a little coal oil left in the reservoir. He bound together a torch of meadow grass hay, soaked it with what coal oil was left, and again snapped a Lucifer into life.

It lit immediately, and he walked from stall to stall, hay stack to stack, and got them all going. They had one old mare that had been on the place for years and was past doing anything but digesting meadow grass, and he turned her out, slapped her on the rump, and watched her trot out of the barn. As he did the mare, he walked to the hen house and freed the dozen red hens and the rooster.

They was on their own now, just as he was.

The cabin was fully involved in the bedroom and the flames had burned through the curtains and the shutters and were licking the outside walls above the windows as he passed, but he didn't bother to look. And he ignored Ranger, who was barking wildly, running back and forth, obviously thinking his master crazed.

And he couldn't argue with the dog. He was crazed and had been for more than a week since Consuela was ravaged and murdered in the bed they'd shared for years.

And he planned to stay crazed until she was avenged, or he was dead.

He mounted and gigged the horse and led the mule to the top of the rise, where a flat carved chunk of sandstone marked her grave.

Here lies the best most beautiful woman to ever love this view, or any other.

He removed his hat but didn't bother to dismount.

"*Vaya con Dios,* my beautiful *señorita.* Rest in peace. I won't be visiting you for a long while, but I know you've gone on to your reward. I'm sorry there wasn't a priest so you could have made your last confession or gotten absolution . . . as I know that was something you believed in."

He had nothing left to say or do, and he felt as if a sword had opened his gut, and all the kindness and compassion he'd ever felt for another human were being poured out onto her grave. As he gigged the horse, he carried nothing with him but anger and revenge. And the dust that now covered his heart, and probably always would.

Then he clamped his jaw so hard it hurt and turned the animals downhill, toward the Yellowstone.

And the Ragged Rock Ridge ranch.

CHAPTER FIVE

Five days after driving out in the buckboard, Hong and his nephew, Choo, returned to the Triple R headquarters. Braddick immediately called him into his library, where he was playing snooker with his foreman.

"So, what did Mrs. McLaughton have to say?"

"Missy McLaughton say thank you, but she happy and son working hard killing coyotes and wolves."

"*Humph,*" Braddick managed, made a bad shot and cursed, then turned back to his cook and housekeeper. "So, did you talk to Ling and anyone else?"

"Ling say sheriff quit—"

"Is the Quiet Waters place up for sale?"

Hong merely shrugged.

"God damn it, Hong, you're not telling me something."

Again, he shrugged, then mumbled something.

"Damn you, speak up."

"Say it for sale, but not to Triple R."

"What? How the hell can he do that?"

"Don' know. It said not sell to Triple R."

"We'll see about that. So, did Reagan go back East?"

Again, Hong shrugged.

"Damn you, man, tell me what you know, or I'll cut that silly queue off'n your head and feed it to the hogs."

"They say he come to Triple R."

Both Braddick and Spike Howard guffawed at that. Then Braddick said, "He's coming here with how many men?"

"No one say other men. Only sheriff . . . but he no longer sheriff. He quit."

"He quit?"

"Quit. Town looking new sheriff."

Spike laughed, then added, "I never figured Reagan for a damn fool, but if he's riding over here alone, and particularly if'n he left his badge behind . . . well, he's a damn fool. He must be blinded by rage, or stupidity. Or wanting to commit suicide and doesn't have the guts to do it himself. We'll accommodate him."

Braddick took a sip of his brandy, then nodded to Spike. "Next time Paddy makes a pass by the home place, you tell him to put the word out to watch out for this 'damn fool.' We don't want him getting lucky and shooting no Triple R riders down." He paused and re-lit his cigar, exhaled a long billow of smoke, then added, "I'll have his place bought in a fortnight, and for a damn sight less than I'd have paid him. This could work out just fine after all. He must truly wanna join his chile pepper in the great beyond if he's riding in here."

Spike made a shot, then looked up. "If he comes near one of us, I'll shoot his balls off, so if he does join up with her, he'll be singing the high notes, and she won't have much use for him."

Both he and Braddick had a good laugh, then went back to their game.

Chapter Six

Quint was normally clean shaven, as a man of the law in a town full of church-going folks should be, but he already had nearly ten days of beard growth going and figured that he didn't need to be easily recognized by the Ragged Rock Ridge bunch, so he'd let it grow and would continue to let hair and beard cover the clean-shaven sheriff he'd been.

That, and a celluloid collar turned backward, might get him in range of some Triple R riders who'd otherwise recognize him.

He wondered if using the image of a God-fearing man to send men to hell would anger the Lord but then had to smile, as he remembered Exodus: "And I will stretch out my hand, and smite Egypt with all my wonders which I will do in the midst thereof: and after that he will let you go." Well, he was on the trail to smite Egypt, only this time Egypt was the Triple R, and he would be letting a number of souls go . . . to the devil if he had his way.

He worked his way down the trail to Buffalo Crossing, where the Yellowstone ran wide and shallow, paused at the bank, and yelled at Ranger and patted the forks of the saddle. It wasn't the first time Ranger had been invited to ride, and he leapt high enough that Quint could catch him by the nape of the neck and hoist him up in front of him. Then he pulled Kit up alongside his buckskin, Adobe, and tied his lead rope back to the packsaddle, knowing the mule would follow. He gigged Adobe and let him have his head as he plunged into the stream. The river was well over a hundred yards across, but it was only horse-belly deep through a channel for twenty-five yards, then only knee deep on the buckskin for the rest of the way. The big horse lunged a couple of times—probably the soft bottom worried him—but then settled and charged forward, flinging water to each side.

Quint glanced behind and was pleased to see Kit was close on their tail as they pulled out and up a trail that was twenty or more paces wide and must have been made by centuries of buffalo. He scratched Ranger's ears, then let him slide to the ground. Barely wet, the dog shook nonetheless as if soaked to the bone, then checked the trail with his nose and moved away at a lope to the north.

The wide bluff trail continued up a long draw until it topped out two hundred feet above the river on top of the bluffs, where the rolling hills were deep in prairie grass and the air smelled of fresh grass and sage, well out of the copse of cottonwood and willows lining the river below. Quint reined Adobe to the side of the wide trail, almost into a patch of sage, and a pair of sage hens broke from the brush and with powerful wing beats gained altitude, then glided two hundred yards and back into another dark covering that marked a ravine that ran almost to the ridge-line.

He had to remember to re-load the scattergun with birdshot. A hen would make a fine supper for him and the pup. And he knew he had to eat, fuel for the task ahead.

Quint spun the horse and reined up, hooked a leg over the horn, and sat for a minute looking back upriver to where he could just see where Quiet Waters topped a ridge south of the river. Smoke rose from behind a hill somewhere below, and he had a pang of regret that all his and Consuela's hard work was now little more than a pile of ash and blackened timbers.

Then he clamped his jaw, spun Adobe, and spurred him into an easy lope. Kit followed, his load bouncing a little precariously, so, even as eager as he was to get this over, Quint reined

Adobe back to a quick single foot. It wouldn't do to have his supplies spread all over the land.

After an hour he began to see cattle grazing . . . to his surprise cattle with the Triple R wiggling brand. He figured he'd ride for at least two days before seeing signs of the Triple R . . . but it seemed the Triple R was growing out of the Judith Basin. Braddick thought he was going to own the world.

Some off these rangy, rough-looking cows had a slight bump between their shoulders, reminiscent of the Mexican cattle Braddick had driven up from Texas ten years ago. Some had the extra horn length that testified to a mixture of longhorn as well.

Braddick had bought a pair of fine bulls from the East a couple of years later, and a dozen Hereford cows the year after that, and now those Mexican brahmas and longhorns were interbred with fine bald-faced Herefords. He kept the first batch of two bulls the cows dropped and now had two dozen fine looking long-loined Hereford bulls spread over the range. He was a good cattleman, but with a sour soul and bad temper that made him a bad neighbor and worse boss. Consequently, he had the worst kind of trash working for him, a few of them known to have ridden with Braddick himself, who'd spent some time with the Union.

In Quint's opinion, most of them were trash, but that didn't mean they weren't a formidable enemy.

Quint himself had been one of few to qualify as a sharp-shooter, and to serve under Colonel Henry A. Post, who commanded the U.S.S.S., the 2nd United States Sharpshooters. In order to be accepted as a sharpshooter, a volunteer was expected to pass a qualifying marksmanship test. A Minnesota newspaper advertised for Sharpshooter recruits who were "able-bodied men used to the rifle." Prospective sharpshooters were expected to shoot "a string of fifty inches in ten consecutive shots at two hundred yards, with globe or telescopic sights from a rest."

None of the bullets were to be more than five inches from the center of the bull. A candidate shooting offhand was required to achieve a fifty-inch string at a distance of one hundred yards, again, nothing over five inches.

Quint shot a two-inch group from a rest and a three-and-a-half-inch offhand. Had his group been a turkey shoot, he'd have taken home the bird.

It was the benefit and result of hunting squirrels and rabbits to fill his mother's larder . . . with a little .30-caliber single-shot muzzleloader from the time he was nine years old.

But, after being accepted into the 2nd, it was the last time he'd see Minnesota. Two years into service, he got word that his parents had both passed, his mother from cholera and his pa only a month later from a horse going over backward on him, so there was nothing to go home to as the farm had been auctioned off to pay debts. But an honest sheriff had sent him a draft for the sixteen hundred dollars left over. Thus, after the war, he came West.

With hope in his heart and money in his pocket.

Unfortunately, his Sharp's carbine remained behind with his regiment, but he wasn't too bad with the .44-40 model 73 Winchester in his saddle scabbard. In fact, it was his habit to shoot deer and antelope, and the occasional elk, in the head at up to two hundred yards, so as not to mess up the meat. He seldom missed.

Just before dark he found a trickle of water working its way out of an east-facing ravine that was lined with a few alder, so green with new foliage it would hurt your eyes, and some lodge-pole pine. He figured the draw for lots of firewood, so it would be a fine place to make a camp. The sun would hit it first thing, and it wasn't so steep a horse couldn't top the ridge at the back, just in case a rider would need a fast, well-covered, exit. When he worked his way up the ravine and dismounted near a small meadow of grass growing tall and green from the trickle, he looked back over his shoulder to see a tendril of smoke a mile or so away. He staked the buckskin and worked his way on foot twenty feet higher up a rock bank until he could see the roof of a soddy and its rock stack where the smoke originated.

Was it a homesteader, or a Triple R line camp? He figured the latter, as Braddick would not tolerate a homestead on what he considered his range . . . even if it was free range.

So it was about to begin.

Chapter Seven

Quint unhooked and set aside the panniers but left the mule saddled in case he needed to make a fast exit, then watered the mule in the trickle and staked him in a patch of grass. He watered Adobe, filled his canteens, wished he had time to cook his beans, but instead checked his weapons and made ready to visit the soddy in the distance.

The sun was settling below the horizon to the west of him, up near the end of the ravine he occupied. All his weapons checked and loaded, he mounted up and gigged Adobe down the trickle, with Ranger padding along behind. The dog was a quiet creature and only barked when Quint needed to be warned of something, so Quint had no trouble with him going along.

He was not surprised when he followed the trickle in the increasing starlight—the moon was yet to rise—and followed as it circled a hill and headed directly toward where he knew the soddy to be. It made sense they'd build near water. A few willows lined the trickle, and soon he saw light working its way out of cracks between closed shutters.

Tying Adobe to a thicker than normal willow branch, he slipped the Winchester from the scabbard and hoisted the Smith and Wesson to make sure it rode free and easy, then turned to the pup. Speaking very low, he motioned the dog to lie down.

"Ranger, you stay. Stay with Adobe." Then he turned and padded slowly and as silently as possible until he was at the uphill
back wall. It rose only two feet above the roof—a deep growth
of grass covered the sod—as it was dug into the hillside. Had
you come to it from above, you'd hardly see it.

The soft sod and grass made for a quiet approach to the
stone chimney, and he moved slowly there, removed his coat,
and draped it over the smoking opening.

Then he lay down on the edge of the roof, not far above and
just to the side of the door.

In less than a minute, the door swung aside, flooding the
ground with light, and a man stumbled out, coughing and
wheezing . . . and, to Quint's surprise, he was followed closely
by a woman, rubbing her eyes with the apron she wore and
coughing as well. Neither of them appeared to be armed.

Quint zeroed the muzzle of the Winchester on the man and
called out. "Pilgrim, raise your hands. Lady, you, too."

"What, what?" the man mumbled in a slightly high voice,
then in the light flooding from inside, Quint realized he was
little more than a boy.

The woman yelled at him. "You take that obstruction off that
opening right this instant."

Quint couldn't help but smile, then said in a low tone, "Lady,
you've got a lot of sand for a person staring into the business
end of a Winchester."

"And you're no kind of a gentleman, bothering a peaceful
mother and son about to say their nightly prayers. Remove that
cloth, this instant."

"I'll oblige you but don't move from that spot."

The boy spoke for the first time as Quint moved over to
recover his coat. "Ma, be careful. We don't know who this owlhoot is."

"I'm jumping down over here. You two stay put."

Quint moved to where the drop was only four feet or so and dropped down, out of sight of the pair.

He rounded the front corner.

The boy was still coughing and hacking, but the woman was gone. By the time he sidled up next to the boy, only shoulder high to him, a voice rang out from the doorway.

The smoke inside was rapidly clearing, and Quint had no problem seeing the woman backlit and holding an old double barrel leveled at his chest. And she handled it as if she were no stranger to the weapon.

He moved a couple of inches closer, and slightly behind the boy, who still hacked away and tried to rub the smoke out of his eyes.

Quint again smiled and spoke in a low, even tone. "Lady, you cut loose with that old blunderbuss and you'll surely blow me in half, but you'll blow a hell of a chunk out of this boy as well. You want that?"

He moved to where he was even more shielded by the boy as she hesitated.

"Move away from him," she instructed the boy, but Quint encircled his throat with a forearm.

"He ain't going nowhere, lady. Not so long as you got that cannon aimed our way."

"What are you doing here?"

Quint decided to take another tack. "Ma'am, you're on Triple R land. The question is, what are *you* doing here?"

She lowered the muzzle a foot, looking puzzled. "You're with the Triple R?"

Quint didn't quite lie, but he did nod and reply, "Ma'am."

"We're working for the Triple R." The muzzle came down and buried itself in the folds of her skirt. "Why'd you try and smoke us out?"

"Ma'am, I didn't just try, I did smoke you out. I thought you were someone trying to homestead on Triple R land. Mr. Braddick wouldn't take kindly to that."

"I'm sure he wouldn't," she said, and Quint couldn't help but notice the sour look that came over her, but she stepped aside from the doorway.

"Has it cleared?" the boy asked, his eyes still tearing.

"Yes. Mister, you care for some coffee? I've got a cup or so left from my nightly."

"Yes, ma'am, I surely would."

She waved him in, and the boy followed.

It was about as simple a place as it could be, like so many from Nebraska this way. There were only two rooms, the back one holding a four-poster double bed, with a canopy hung from post to post to keep the dirt and mealy bugs from dropping down, and the front a decent flat-top potbellied stove in addition to the fireplace, a table and four chairs, a few shelves hung from the log walls, and a pie safe—little other accouterments, but the place was well swept and spotless as a woman could keep it with a hard dirt floor and no rugs.

There was a pot from a swing-arm over the coals in the firebox of the stone fireplace and a coffee pot on the potbellied stove. She grabbed up a tin cup and a towel for a hot pad and poured him a steaming cup, full to the brim. The place smelled of smoke but more and more with the odor of something that made his mouth water filling the room and his nostrils.

The table was only door-wide and equally as long with four ladder-back chairs with woven hemp seats someone, sometime, had brought from the East, and she sat in one and motioned him to the other. The boy took a seat on one, pulling it near the potbellied stove.

"Obliged," Quint said, then burned his lips trying to take a sip.

"Sorry, it's hot. You got a name, stranger?" she asked.

"Dang near everbody does," he said, with a bit of a twinkle in his eye, but she obviously didn't see the humor, so he added, and lied, "Smith. Willard Smith, but folks call me Will."

"How come we didn't meet you down at the home place, Will Smith. We were there most of a month before Tommy here took this job."

"I work the line camps. Been tending the new calves over to the southwest. So, what's Tommy's job?"

The boy spoke up. "I'm killing coyotes when I come on them . . . I'm a real good shot . . . and poisoning and shootin' wolves. Lots of wolves over on this side of the Judith. They take lots of calves. And I get to keep the hides and get as much as a buck apiece for them . . . or so I'm told."

Quint couldn't help but frown. "That's a dirty business, son. I hope you're being real careful with all that?"

The woman answered. "I hate the work, but we had to take it. We lost everything . . . got robbed out on the trail. Mr. Braddick wanted us to stay on at the home place, but I was . . ." She hesitated for a long moment before continuing, then added, ". . . uncomfortable there, so here we are. He did give Tommy a fine rifle to use."

For the first time Quint really looked at her and realized under the worry and concern of having a stranger literally drop in, she was a beautiful and fairly young woman somewhat hidden under a dust cap: hair blond, eyes blue, trim of waist yet buxom. He was surprised he noticed as Consuela had not even been gone two weeks . . . and he thought he'd never be able to look at a woman again. He felt a twinge of guilt.

He couldn't help but ask, "You Tommy's sister?"

That made her smile. "No, no, I'm his mother." She nodded demurely. "I'm Sarah McLaughton . . ." then quickly added, "Mrs. Sarah McLaughton."

Finally able to drink the coffee, he downed half of it and rose to his feet. "Well, Mrs. McLaughton, I'm sorry to have troubled you and Tommy. I'll take my leave now and leave you to your evening prayers."

"We've got a lean-to down closer to the creek, where there's our old mules stabled. If you need a place to bed down out of the weather . . . at least out of the rain . . ."

"No, ma'am. I'm camped over yonder and have some stock there."

"Have you had your supper?"

"No need for that, ma'am. I'm sure you need what you have way out here."

"I have a pot full of what God provides. We have half that pot left"—she motioned at a gallon-size iron pot hanging over the coals—"full of sage hen, a couple of turnips, and wild onions. We've got a root cellar full of potatoes and carrots and turnips. We're fine. You set back down and fill your belly."

She was adamant, and his gut was growling, and he wasn't of a mind to turn down what he'd been smelling.

"Your wish is my command, ma'am."

She smiled at that. "You sound like a man of the mountains, and then again like an educated man from the East. Which is it, Mr. Smith?"

He changed the subject. "So, if you don't mind my asking, where's Mr. McLaughton?"

She and the boy both spoke at once. The boy said, "He's kilt," and at the same time, she said, "Out on the prairie."

Quint cleared his throat. "I'm no threat to you, Mrs. McLaughton."

She gave him a tight smile. "Mr. Smith, it's not what a man says, it's what he does."

"You have no reason to tell me a . . ." *Lie,* he started to say, then said, "Falsehood."

She eyed him carefully, then cleared her throat and said, "Put it back down on that chair. I'm feeding you."

"And I'm proud to oblige. I'll not prevaricate."

"Like I said, an educated man."

Chapter Eight

He was up in time to see the first shafts of light cut the sky to the east, under a high flat overcast as tabletop-even on its bottom as a flat iron, and almost as dark. Were Quint a betting man he'd bet on a hard, steady rain before the day was out.

As he watered Adobe and Kit, he couldn't help but wonder what Mrs. McLaughton and her boy were about to have for breakfast. Whatever it was, he'd wager it was way more tasty than the hunk of mule deer jerky he and Ranger gnawed on.

They moved out at a steady walk, northwest, toward the Triple R headquarters. After three hours, he made out another tendril of smoke, hard to see against the gray sky, but it was there, and it was likely another Triple R line camp. As he got closer and closer, he threaded his way through cattle, all with the brand he was coming to hate.

The country was wide flats of grass cut with sharp, deep ravines, a few with muddy, slow-moving water, but he was able to find trails where the cattle had made their way up and down. As he neared the rising smoke, he eyed the mountain that rose behind. Thick with alder down low, backed up by a heavy copse of lodgepole, then lodgepole mixed with ponderosa until it played out on talus slopes and hard-shouldered granite that rose high enough to be treeless and surrounded by cloud. He figured the mountain was the highest for miles. When the smoke was a half mile away, he moved up into the alders.

When he figured he was even with the source of the smoke, he turned back east along the first trickle of water. The first meadow he came to, he dropped the panniers from Kit's packsaddle and hobbled him where he had lots of graze. Again, he motioned Ranger down and checked his weapons before he remounted and let Adobe pick his way down through the alders, working around blowdown.

The alders thinned well before he got near what proved to be a long log cabin, at least twice the size of the McLaughton soddy. A lean-to up against the back of the cabin held six horses. A quarter of it was filled with meadow hay, and a small covered area served as a tack room and held what looked to be a grain bin. Another twenty paces away was a privy, but without walls, only four poles with cross braces and a six-by-six-foot roof to keep the rain off those doing their business. It was little more than a covered bench with a hole in it. Between the privy and the house, a small single-horse buckboard rested, its harness piled on the seat. Its bed was piled with sacks of flour and other dry goods, some of which were covered with canvas.

He tied Adobe a hundred yards back in the trees, now thick with new growth, and out of sight of the cabin. Then, carrying his Winchester with his Smith and Wesson Russian on his hip and a Colt in hand, he picked his way until he found a pile of boulders and brush only forty yards from the place.

Then he settled in to watch, covered by a low-growing chokecherry tree.

The same trickle of water was wider now—a half-dozen feet across where it passed fifty feet from the cabin. The sun was already behind the mountain behind him when a man with a full beard walked out of the cabin, carrying a bucket, and made his way to the creek. He filled it and returned until he disappeared around the front of the cabin. Quint puzzled on it but didn't recognize the man fetching water.

He heard the door slam but still waited.

Light was fading when he saw three riders approaching at a lope, eager, he figured, to get there in time for supper. The smoke from the stone chimney had increased, and he caught the occasional whiff of bacon frying.

The riders came to the rear of the cabin, unsaddled and stowed their gear, put up the horses, and turned to head for the front. And, for the first time, Quint got a good look at one of them as the man snatched his hat off.

Quint felt the heat flood his backbone as he recognized the one they called Skunk.

CHAPTER NINE

The stripe of white hair front to back on top his head gave the killer away as much as if he'd called out his name.

Having no interest in being a bushwhacker, although he'd shot many a man from a long distance during the war, he did not shoulder the Winchester.

War was war . . . this was something else. Besides, he wanted to look the men he would kill in the eye and see their fear and pain close up.

However, he had no interest in banging on the door and asking for supper, as his beard was less than a half inch, and there was the slight chance more than one of them had been in town while he was doing his duty as sheriff; it wouldn't do to be recognized. Folks had a tendency to remember the face behind the badge.

No, he'd bide his time. Besides, it wasn't a prudent man who charged into any situation with his back burning with anger and his mind flooded red with revenge.

He made himself sit back and relax. Finally, in the cold darkness with only the stars lighting his way, he worked his way back to the meadow where Kit and Ranger waited and built a tiny fire. The beans had been soaking for two days and cooked easily in his small cast-iron skillet, and he added a handful of jerky and a handful of watercress he'd picked from the bank of the trickle. It wasn't bad, but it wasn't Mrs. McLaughton or Consuela.

He'd always been able to set an internal alarm clock and did so, awaking at four a.m. or so he figured by the stars and the fact the moon was already heading down in the west. It had rained hard sometime during the night, and most of his gear was wet, but he'd covered up with a canvas pack cover and had managed to stay dry.

He finished his stew for breakfast, eating it cold and not bothering with a fire, sharing it with the dog. One more chore: he again found a rock pile and hid a small stash of beans, flour, and jerky. Only then did he saddle up and move back to his pile of boulders, leaving the animals only thirty yards or so behind in case he needed a quick retreat.

The sun had been up for a half hour when four men exited the cabin. One of them headed for the privy, the other three relieved themselves, then moved to the tack and saddled up.

Skunk was currying a dun-colored gelding. Quint made note of the fact he had no long arm, only a sidearm. All of the men had lariats on their saddles, but only Skunk and one other had a bedroll behind the saddle. Quint figured they were leaving for at least an overnight, if not returning to the home place.

While they were saddling, a fifth man with a full beard again took the bucket to the stream.

Quint figured five was it, and, the best he could tell from his hideout, only one of them was a target.

The two without bedrolls rode out to the south, and Skunk and another man, one with a prodigious belly, mounted up and headed north.

He decided to bide his time and, as he would have during the war, reconnoiter his situation. He'd risk approaching the house. Moving back to the animals he dug into his pack and came up with the celluloid collar. It was time to preacher up.

After all four riders were out of sight, he mounted and rode up to the front of the cabin, dismounted, and tied the animals to a hitching rail.

"Hello the house," he yelled out, and a man came to the door, opening it wide, unarmed. He was expecting no trouble.

"Howdy," he called out. "Come on in."

Quint headed in and got four feet from the door when the bearded man eyed his collar and asked, "You a travelling preacher?"

"Yes, sir. Travelling from Nebraska all the way to Helena, where I understand there are plenty of sinners."

The man laughed, scratched under his arm, where there was a hole in the one-piece union suit he wore under a pair of canvas pants—he hadn't bothered with a shirt—and waved him on inside. "Hell, Preacher, there's no lack of sinners anywhere on God's good earth."

Quint nodded in agreement. He noticed the man had on low-heeled brogans, not the foot-ware of a man who spent time in the saddle.

The man grabbed a pot of coffee off a Buck stove and motioned to Quint to take a seat, and as he poured a crockery cup full asked, "You had your breakfast, Preacher?"

"Had a mouthful or so. I'm running a bit low on grub." It was a lie, but he wanted an excuse to parley with the man a while and learn what he could.

"Well, sir, I'm happy to have the company. The rest of the boys rode out a while back. I've got a few biscuits and a pot of honey, if you're interested. I'm Paddy O'Brady . . . You're on the Triple R, and will be for at least two days ride west, if you're interested."

"What's that mouth waterin' smell?" Quint asked.

"Got a dozen loafs of bread in the oven," Paddy replied with a broad grin.

163

As Quint sipped his coffee, he smiled to himself. This man was a talker, and he figured he'd hang around a while and pick his brain. The rain had wet the prairie, and he'd have no trouble getting on Skunk's trail and hopefully staying on it until he found him alone.

Paddy made a fine biscuit, and Quint told him so.

"So, Mr. O'Brady, you the boss of this outfit?" Quint asked.

That brought a guffaw from Paddy. "I'm about as far as a body can get from being the bossman. I'm a line cook. We got a half-dozen line shacks just like this one, each one housing a half-dozen or so hands. I make the rounds from shack to shack, whipping up lots of bread and hard tack and pots of stew and beans, and occasionally oatmeal cookies and a few pies if we ain't run out of dried apples. I rest a day, visit the home place and restock, then start all over again."

"So, this Triple R . . . a fine place to work?"

Paddy was silent for a moment as his face fell, then he said, "Some fine fellas, some stink like the south end of a northbound skunk and is mean as rattlesnakes."

"And the bossman?"

"Mr. Bradford Braddick."

"And, which kind is he?" Just the sound of the man's name brought the taste of bile to Quint's throat.

"Fella shouldn't talk about the man pays his wages."

Quint smiled. "Well, Paddy, that's admirable, but you can tell your preacher."

That made Paddy smile. "Fact is, he's a rotten son-of-a-bitch, but if'n you run into him, don't mention I said so."

The preacher smiled and lied. "I doubt if I'll be running into him. How about the rest of the boys . . . they all ride for the brand?"

"Most are just hands needing the thirty bucks a month and found. A few . . . a half dozen maybe . . . followed old man

Braddick back here after the war, and they are a bad lot. He's got them cut out to do his dirty work, and he's had more than his share for them to do."

A half dozen? What a coincidence. For the first time, Quint's memory niggled him, and the name Braddick banged around in his head until he came up with a story he'd heard, many years ago.

"Braddick . . . seems I remember a colonel who resigned his commission after a payroll came up missing. Nothing could be proved, but he resigned as I heard it before he could be drummed out. An Ohio colonel and outfit, if'n I recall."

"That would be one and the same. As I hear'd it—and it ain't much talked about around any Triple R campfire—Bradford Braddick arrived in Montana with a bag full of paper money. But he worked some of the boomtowns for a while so he could say where he come by it . . . gold, that is. He bought gold in lots of mining camps, trading paper money. Funny thing was, he paid for lots of supplies and such with good old American paper money. It was like he was trying to get rid of the paper."

"And this ex-army crew of his . . . they work cattle?"

"Ha . . . fact is, they ramrod the line camps making sure all the hands are working cattle. They's almost always one of them at one line camp or another."

Quint looked around as if he doubted Paddy's words.

So Paddy spoke up.

"Hell, one of them, Skunk Tobias, left here not more'n an hour ago. Headed over to Dead Squaw Canyon camp just around the mountain."

Quint had one more thing that interested him, so he asked. "I met a nice lady and her son back south of here aways. She with the Triple R?"

"Mrs. McLaughton and Tommy. Good folks. Her husband

was killed out on the trail by some owlhoots, and they robbed their outfit leaving 'em afoot, and she and Tommy was taken in by Braddick . . . until there was some kind of trouble betwixt 'em, and she said she had to leave. Braddick didn't want her to go, so he offered Tommy a job to keep them on the place. They didn't have a pot to piss in . . . pardon the expression, Preacher."

"What kind of trouble?"

"She's a handsome woman, as I'm sure you noticed. No one knows but Sarah and Braddick, but I imagine he was sniffin' around like the dirty old hound dog he is. And her just newly widowed an' all."

Quint changed the subject again. "So, where was this Skunk fella heading again? Maybe I might catch up and ride along."

"I'm sure they have too large a head start. However, he's headed to Dead Squaw, the next line camp to the west. Stay at the base of the mountain until it turns west, and ride about ten miles until you come to a creek that's twenty paces across. Turn downstream aways, and you'll come on the camp. It's some bigger than here with gathering pens that'll hold two or three hundred head."

"I may stop, or I may just ride on."

"Lee Yong is the housekeeper there and the daily cook for a dozen men who bunk there. All I do is bake when I swing by. Most the men call him Young Lee, or just by his surname, Lee. He cooks a fine mess of chicken . . . they got a big hutch over there . . . and I'm sure would feed you."

"Who else bunks there? Who runs that part of the outfit?"

"Some Irish trash my people would have run out of County Cork. With luck, he and Skunk will be off hunting for camp meat. Which means pulling a cork, telling each other lies, and laying on their butts out of sight of the big boss . . . or anyone who might sing that song to Braddick."

"In case he is there, does he have a name?"

"Shamus O'Shawnnaessy, a sheep fu— sheep-mounting fool who'd breed a pile of brush if he thought a snake resided therein, but a mean son-of-a-bitch, if you'll pardon my language, Preacher. No offense meant."

"None taken. So long as there's no ladies in earshot. However, I wish you'd say what you feel about the man!" Then Quint had a really good bellylaugh for the first time since he'd come on the terrible sight of his wife.

Quint had finished his biscuits, so he rose and extended his hand. "Paddy, it's been a real pleasure. Hope the good Lord smiles on you . . . I believe he would on any man makes as good a biscuit as you do even if he doesn't hit his knees regular. Wish I could hang around for a taste of that bread I've been smellin'."

"Well, Preacher, I'll tell you what I'm gonna do. They is coming out of the oven in about a minute and a half, by that hourglass over yonder. You can just take a loaf with you to enjoy on your journey. These no-goods 'round here won't miss it."

"That's mighty Christian of you, Paddy."

"You put in a good word with the Old Man for me."

"You can count on it," Quint said.

With a fresh loaf in his saddlebag, Quint mounted and gave Paddy a friendly goodbye wave, then set off to collect his mule and pup.

Now it was time to get to work, tracking Skunk Tobias until he was alone or with this Irish Shamus trash and either or both ready to meet Satan and his fire and fork.

CHAPTER TEN

As Quint suspected the trail was clear and easily followed.

On the path Paddy had suggested, he followed two shod horses that were moving at a comfortable walk. So he picked up the pace. At the first small creek he came to, he reined upstream and into a line of lodgepole up on a shelf, where he found a flat meadow with lots of graze and where the little stream ponded behind some enterprising beavers.

He unsaddled Kit and hid the panniers and packsaddle in a wind cave at the base of a sandstone face, quickly covering them with rocks and brush. Hobbling the mule, he told Ranger to stay with the animal, encouraging him with a chunk of the fresh bread and a handful of jerky. He stuffed a couple of pints of whiskey, some jerky, the rest of the bread, and one sack of coffee in his saddlebags and mounted.

Then he returned to the trail and set Adobe into a steady lope. He meant to catch up with the pair and not wait until the unlikely situation of finding Skunk and Shamus off in the woods emptying a jug.

After two hours of alternating riding at a lope for a mile, then walking a quarter mile, he topped a rise and started another walking part of his pursuit . . . when he heard a gunshot in the distance. He reined up and listened. But no shots followed.

He put Adobe into an easy pace that was a natural gait for him, moving quickly but not tiring him as a lope or gallop would, then spotted the men in the distance. They had an antelope hanging from the limb of a large chokecherry on the banks of the shallow twenty-stride-wide creek Paddy had said to look for.

The good news was he'd caught up, the bad that the line camp and who knows how many men were only a mile or two downstream.

Quint pulled the Winchester from his scabbard and laid it across his thighs, then moved forward at a walk. He saw that the fat man glanced over his shoulder and saw him coming but paid little attention and went back to his task, skinning the antelope doe.

He still had the collar on in the preacher fashion and was

within fifty feet of them when Skunk looked up and snapped, "Had you moved a little faster, stranger, you could have helped with this critter and been entitled to some of the roast we're about to enjoy."

"How about I throw in some fresh bread and a bottle of whiskey. Does that make my company more appealing?"

"It does, but who the hell are you, and what's your business on the Triple R?"

"I'm the Reverend Will Smith, out from Omaha, on my way to Helena to save souls."

The fat man guffawed, then offered, "They damn sure got plenty need saving. You say you got a bottle of whiskey?"

"I do."

"Then we'll roast the backstraps and a chunk of butt while we enjoy a few slugs of your jug, if that suits you?"

"Ha," Skunk said with a snarl. "If it suits you or don't suit you. Get down from that nag and produce this bottle you brag about."

Quint dismounted without taking his eyes off the pair, and without slipping the Winchester back into its scabbard. He'd loaded the scattergun with a pair of double aught shells, and it was stuffed in the center of his bedroll and easily extracted, but he was well heeled so didn't feel the need. He dug into his saddlebag, pulled the cork from the jug of whiskey with his teeth, handing it over to Skunk.

But Skunk didn't reach; he was studying Quint.

"Don't I know you, Preacher?"

"Have you ever been to the Lutheran Church in Omaha?"

Skunk was frowning like he'd just sucked a lemon. "That ain't where I know you from . . . and hell, no, I ain't never been to no Lutheran God-wallow. I don't go to my knees for anyone or thing . . . God included."

We'll see about that, Quint thought but didn't say.

The fat man wiped his knife on his pants and moved forward. "You two can palaver until the moon rises, but I'm gonna try that jug of Black Widow." He reached, grabbed the jug, and upended it, taking a full mouthful.

"Damn you," snapped Skunk, reaching for the jug. "They didn't nickname you Hogman Harry for nothing. Give me that." He jerked the jug out of the fat man's hands, eliciting a frown from him.

"Take a mouthful and hand it back," he snapped.

"Your name is Harry?" Quint asked.

"Handsome Harry Hanover, the scourge of most of the fair and fat soiled doves of Montana. And you're?"

"Again, I'm the Reverend Will Smith, recently of Omaha."

He eyed Skunk, who had the jug upended as Quint answered, then glanced his way. "I hope you got another jug."

"So happens I do, so you fellows go ahead and down that one." Quint walked to the other side of Adobe and dug into the other saddlebag, producing another bottle. When Skunk saw that, he handed the almost empty jug back to Hogman, who drained it.

Since Skunk was the object of his intentions, he pulled the cork from the new jug and ignored the reaching fat man, handing it to him. And Skunk obliged, tipping it up and swallowing three or four mouthfuls.

Then he backhanded the dribble from his chin and belched loudly. Again, eyeing Quint, he got a look of recognition.

"Hell's bells, I know you . . ." He reached for the six-gun on his hip.

But he was an instant slow, as the muzzle of Quint's Winchester had only to move a foot, and its hammer pulled back, to blow a hole in the center of Skunk's chest. The roar of the Winchester reverberated up the canyon the creek poured out of. As Skunk backpedaled, his eyes went wide and his arms windmilled. Then he caught himself and stumbled forward, with both hands on the hole in his chest. He sunk to his knees, wide eyed, blood beginning to trickle from the sides of his mouth.

Quint ignored him and turned his attention to the fat man as he levered in another shell. Hogman's mouth was hanging open as if he were a beached carp gasping for air. Quint swung the muzzle to bear on the fat man's chest. Hogman had a hand on the butt of a heavy revolver at his waist but realized there was no reason to try unless he was ready to die.

"Turn around," Quint snapped.

"Ain't right to shoot a man in the back," Hogman muttered.

"Turn around, now," Quint said, again.

And the man did so. Quint brought the heavy barrel of the Winchester down on top of the fat man's pumpkin-sized head, and he dropped to his knees. So Quint brought the next one around from the side, smashing into the fat man's temple, with a thump that could be heard back at the last line camp . . . and this time Hogman crashed to the ground, his arms and legs askew, unmoving.

Skunk was still on his knees, a hand on his revolver, but he didn't seem to have the strength to pull it.

"You didn't want to be on your knees," Quint said and walked forward and kicked Skunk in the chest, and he went to his back.

Skunk managed to get to his side, hacked and spat a mouthful of blood, but couldn't seem to get enough air to do a decent job. Then his arms were thrown out, he rolled to his back, and his eyes went blank. But his chest was still bubbling lung blood from the .44-40 hole, so Quint knew his black heart still beat.

Quint, strangely, felt nothing—no elation, no remorse. He levered in another shell and walked over and said, "This one's for Consuela" and laid the muzzle in the man's crotch and pulled the trigger. He levered in another, bent low and placed the muzzle under Skunk's chin, and blew the top of his head off, including most of his white stripe.

The chest hole stopped bubbling.

Then he drew his knife and cut a *C* in the man's cheek, as big as would fit.

Still, he felt nothing but a sense of satisfaction. He murmured, "One down, Consuela, darling, and six more to go."

He removed the backstraps from the antelope and rolled them and placed them in his saddlebags, then boned out both hindquarters and stowed the meat.

Hogman was moaning, coming to, as Quint reined away heading back to find Kit and Ranger. He was comfortable that Hogman was in no condition to follow and probably couldn't make the ride to the next line camp and its dozen men, even though it was only a couple of miles downstream. He'd be nursing a hell of a headache and whirlpools for eyes for a long time.

Quint would have no pursuers until at least tomorrow, and by that time he'd be on the move. And he knew exactly where he was heading, and it would be a surprise to those who tried to follow.

The hell of it was, now the rest of the Triple R would be on the lookout for a preacher man on a buckskin.

He probably should have put Handsome Harry's lights out forever and saved a lot of soiled doves from acting like Harry was Handsome so they could pry an extra dollar out of his poke, and saved himself from having the Triple R be on the lookout . . . but he wasn't out to punish the innocent, even though he doubted Harry qualified.

If the man had a whisper of a brain, he'd thank the good Lord with every breath he had left.

It was after noon before Quint packed up and, rather than head down to the more established trail, turned back up the mountain.

His plan was to make a wide and very difficult crossing of the mountain, stay shy of any well-used trails, skipping a line camp or two and going on to a distant one—one whose occupants were less likely to be on the lookout for the ex-sheriff of Big Horn.

CHAPTER ELEVEN

Quint only rode his back trail for a quarter mile, until he came to the edge of the canyon that the wide stream flowed from, then turned southwest and into the lodgepole, moving up the canyon. There were lots of blowdown at first, and the going was tough, Adobe having to jump downed timber and weave through the stand of live.

Eventually they rode at the base of a hundred-foot-high escarpment, and Quint worried for a while that he was trapping himself in a box canyon. Ahead he could see a forty-foot-high waterfall; not a good sign.

But he pressed on and found a well-worn but narrow game trail and followed it to the top of the granite and into some jagged uplifts that he wondered might have been the ragged rocks the ranch was named for—ancient rocks full of shells and even the occasional outline of what looked to be marine animals from a time the rocks lay at the bottom of a sea. Some rose to needle points, some to knife-like edges, but between them were wide trail-like openings, and soon he was out of them and onto a wide shelf of towering firs, the forest floor occluded by ferns.

He moved up and up, climbing still, until the firs gave way to rock shelves only occasionally spotted with trees, most whitebark pines.

Adobe's ears shot forward, and he stopped, stiff legged in the trail before the crown of a small ridge ahead. Quint had learned long ago to heed the warning of his animals, but he gigged the big horse forward so he could see ahead. Topping the little crown, it was obvious why the horse was nervous. Across the draw, only a hundred yards away, a large griz was pulling down a white-bark pine to get at a few of last year's seeds. As a griz can outrun a horse in a hundred yards, Quint could understand and appreciate Adobe's reluctance to advance. But the griz winded them, turned his large head to find them with his poor eyesight, then dropped from the tree; Quint was happy to see the animal's big butt as it quickly topped the next rise and disappeared out of sight. A pair of Clark's nutcrackers took up the bear's position in the tree and sassed the horse and rider as they passed.

He'd been riding on rock for the better part of a mile, above the tree line.

Only then, with his trail almost impossible to follow, did he turn back due south, staying in the firs and then on fairly flat shelves of solid granite. He jumped mule deer and one herd of over a dozen bighorn sheep.

He'd taken a route that would take him three times as long to return to his rig and animals, but one that only an expert tracker who recognized fresh nicks in granite could possibly follow.

It was nearly dark before he reined Adobe into the rising moon and back down the mountain, and he figured it was midnight, Quint dozing in the saddle, when the horse found his way back to the beaver pond and Kit and Ranger.

The big buckskin had earned a good night's rest, and Quint hobbled him and let him have his way in the belly-deep grass of the meadow, where Kit grazed contentedly.

Quint fetched his gear from the wind cave, fed the dog a handful of jerky, then rolled in a pack cover with Ranger beside him. He slept the sleep of the contented for the first time since Consuela had been murdered. He had a smile on his face, wondering if Handsome Harry or those from the line camp who found Skunk would have any idea what the *C* carved in Skunk's face represented.

Before he was through with the rest of them, they'd damn well fear the man who carved a *C* in the cheeks of his victims . . . no, in the cheeks of those who'd chosen their fate, by their heinous cowardly actions.

He awoke content for the first time since . . . and in no hurry to ride out. He built an overly large fire and a rack of willow branches and grilled the backstraps and smoked strips of meat sliced from the antelope hindquarters.

He and Ranger ate their fill, then he rode out to the east, back toward the main trail, but only until he came on to the first rock ledge, then turned south, then back east, up the canyon, back to the high country.

If there was one thing he learned in the war, and many times since: a man, or any critter hunted, would win the chase if he did the totally unsuspected.

So he would not ride on to the next line camp, or the one after that. He'd go to a distant camp where they'd most likely not been warned of the threat of a crazy preacher or a crazed widower.

What was beginning to build from his loins up his backbone was the fact he knew that by working his way to the top, he'd instill fear in Braddick. As more men died, he'd know what was coming, what his own fate would be. A quick death from a long-range shooter would be far too good for him, or his secondo, Spike Howard, who actually led the craven cowards who'd ravaged his wife and desecrated his home.

He wanted them to suffer, for a long time.

Picking his way across a wide escarpment of shale, he saw another tendril of smoke in the distance, maybe a quarter mile away, beyond a thicket of fir over a hundred feet tall.

Letting Adobe pick the trail, he moved forward until he

figured he was halfway, then tied the animals and moved on foot. He was sure it was not another line camp but could be a temporary camp of Triple R riders hunting strays.

He dispelled that thought as soon as he saw the source of the smoke—a large fire for an Indian camp, in the center of a ring of six teepees. Watching from the brush at the edge of the meadow they occupied, a smile crossed his face. Indians were supposed to be on the reservations, particularly the Sioux, but reservation life wasn't for Two Hatchets and his immediate band. Quint slung his Winchester muzzle down and holstered his Smith and Wesson Russian, then boldly strode into camp.

First seen by a pair of young women who were filling pots with water at a small stream, they left at a run, leaving pots behind.

By the time he reached the edge of the teepee circle, Two Hatchets and five other braves waited, arms folded. Two Hatchets wasn't giving to smiling but now carried a tight smile and waved Quint forward.

"You are far from Quiet Waters," the war chief said.

"Forever," Quint replied and got a frown from his friend. So he added, "My woman is dead, killed by a band of raiders from the Triple R ranch, and I ride to avenge her."

"Avenge?" Two Hatchets asked, not recognizing the word.

"To bring my weapons against those who killed her."

"Is it help you seek?" he asked, his frown deepening.

"The Sioux have had enough trouble from the white eye. It is only your friendship I seek."

"Easily given, to a friend," Two Hatchets said and smiled tightly again.

"I must retrieve my animals," Quint said.

"My young men will find your animals and bring them in. You must come to the fire with me and smoke."

Quint nodded and followed Two Hatchets, who waved a pair

of young men over and gave them instructions. They left at a trot. Quint yelled after them, "The dog, his name is Ranger." One of the boys waved over his shoulder as they disappeared into the firs.

Quint and Two Hatchets were only halfway through the pipe when the young men reappeared, looking a little sheepish.

They spoke to Two Hatchets, who smiled and turned to Quint. "They say dog more wolf than dog. Would not let them approach."

Quint rose and stretched. "I'll fetch the critters. Tell them I'm sorry and glad they weren't bitten, and glad they didn't hurt my dog, who was doing his job."

Two Hatchets nodded and repeated his apology.

When Quint returned, Two Hatchets waved him into his teepee. "You share my shelter while you with us."

"I have had trouble already, and a man has felt my weapons. They may be following me, but I have been very careful. But they may follow, and I don't want to bring trouble to your camp. I will only stay to rest a while."

"You will stay until you wish to continue your . . . your avenge. My young men backtrack you until they find spot where the trail can be seen far and warn us if men follow."

"Thank you. Then I will sleep for awhile."

"Do, then we eat; we have maize and buffalo, and this little stream full of fish . . . then we dance. As you a guest, I will have the women roast a tongue."

Quint smiled, then rolled in a thick buffalo robe and was asleep in a heartbeat.

Killing could wait.

CHAPTER TWELVE

Paddy O'Brady stood, hat in one hand, his other scratching deep in his beard.

Brad Braddick sat at his rolltop desk, a cigar clamped in his mouth, his brow furrowed. He ran a hand through his full mane of gray hair and eyed Paddy.

"So, this fella that dropped by . . . you say was a travelling preacher?"

"Said he was, had the collar and all."

"You ever see the sheriff in Big Horn?"

"Three or four years—"

"Reagan's only been sheriff there a little over two."

"Then I ain't seen him."

"You say this fella was riding a buckskin?"

"Yes, sir."

"Was he heeled?"

"Not bodily. Howsomever he had a gunsmith's shop on his critters: a sidearm hanging on his saddle horn, a pair of hoglegs in saddle holsters, a long gun in a scabbard, and one rolled in his bed."

"That don't much sound like a preacher to me."

"Well, boss, even preachers have to stay alive out here on the prairie . . . what with renegade Indians runnin' wild and grizzlies and wolves wantin' a chunk outta a man's hide. The way I hear'd it, God helps them who help themselves. A man's gotta be ready, even a preacher man. He seemed like a decent fella . . ."

As he finished, another man rapped on the doorjamb, filled the door with his over-generous frame, and entered.

"What's the problem, Harry?" Braddick asked.

Handsome Harry Hanover, known as Hogman to his bunkmates, grabbed his hat off his head and held it in front. "Some crazy man done shot Skunk dead."

"Who done it, and where?" Braddick asked, standing quickly, and chomping down on his cigar.

"Some wild-eyed preacher wandered into where we was

178

dressing an antelope and just drawed down on Skunk afore he had any chance."

Braddick turned to Paddy. "A decent fella you say?"

Paddy merely shrugged and looked a little sheepish.

Braddick turned back to Hogman. "Riding a big buckskin?"

"That's the fella."

"And what the hell did you do . . . stand there lookin' fat and stupid?"

Hogman pointed to the knot on the side of his head. "He had the drop on us, boss. He made me turn around and whacked me a good one. I musta been out an hour or more. Woke up and he'd stripped the good cuts outta the 'lope and was gone. He was a crazy man. He blowed a hole in Skunk's chest, then blowed his personals away, then put one under his chin. And he carved up his face, laying open a curve like he was a'branding him. All that for the prime cuts of some damn old antelope . . ."

Braddick gritted his teeth, incensed. "That was no preacher. I'd bet a dollar to a donut it's that Reagan fella, and y'all brought him down on us like the plague. I'm surrounded by damn worthless fools." Braddick walked to the doorway to the kitchen and yelled. "Hong, get Spike in here."

"Yes, boss," a voice rang out, and a door slammed. Braddick returned to his desk and plopped down.

"Harry," he snapped, "you get back to your camp. Is Tall Horse still there?"

"He was out hunting wolves."

"Send him here. We got some hunting to do, and it ain't wolves. And we need a tracker."

In moments, a tall, lanky man entered. He didn't bother to remove his hat and wore a strapped down Colt low on the right side.

"Yep," he said, putting a booted foot up on a ladder-back

chair aside Braddick's desk.

"Put the crew together. We got a shit-pile of trouble, and it's your bloody fault."

"What the hell did I do?" Spike, the Triple R foreman, asked with a snarl.

"You let Terror beat that damned Mexican woman to death, and her old man is on a rampage. He killed Skunk with one in the chest, then blew his balls off, then carved up his ugly mug . . . that ain't a man just wanting somebody dead. He wanted revenge, and it's gotta be that Quint Reagan, coming for blood."

"So, let's go get him?"

"Let's? Bullshit. You and the crew track him down. I didn't stick my dong in his woman. And get it done, or don't come back."

"Humph," Spike managed, then snarled, "We'll have his hide tacked to the outhouse wall by the end of the week."

"Make damn sure you do. Seems like the old boy done shook hands with the devil, and a bullet is the only way to cure him of his transgressions. Now get the hell out of here and beat a trail."

"Where's Tall Horse?"

"He's coming. If he ain't here by the time you ride out, I'll have him follow."

"O'Shawnnaessy is over at Lion Cut pushing the hands in the roundup on the side of Bald Mountain. But he ain't much for roping and branding . . . so he'll be riding back soon enough. If he comes in, you send him after us."

"Will do, or if you get anywhere near, send a rider to fetch him if he ain't caught up."

Within an hour, Spike Howard, Torrance "Terror" Oliver, and young Antonio "Tony" Balducci rode out, back to the site of Skunk's killing to pick up a trail. On the way, they ran into the half-Blackfoot, half-Negro Charley Tall Horse, reputed to be the best tracker in Montana. And, within another two hours, they were following the hoofprints of the man who'd shot Skunk dead and blown his personals into the distant mountains.

Shamus O'Shawnnaessy was not only not much for roping and branding, he was even less for doing anything without a bottle of fine Irish mist in his saddlebag, and he was fresh out of whiskey and damned irritated about it. As soon as he made sure the gathering pins at the foot of Baldy Mountain were repaired and the water troughs not leaking more than they were taking in, he decided he could make the ten-plus-mile ride to the Musselshell Trading Post and restock . . . and, besides, there were a couple of fair-haired lasses who worked a room over the plank bar that passed for a saloon next to the pile of rubble that served as a general store and trade-goods cache.

There was a wee lass he'd visited there before—Meagan, if memory served him, and when it came to women it usually did.

He had ten dollars in gold in his pouch, and at a dollar a poke and a dollar for a bottle of Who Hit John, he figured he could spend a couple of days pleasuring Meagan—or any warm, wet female working the post—before he had to return to the roundup. That would give the hands time to gather the damned cows. He'd oversee the branding, then head back to the home place.

Old man Braddick would never know the difference.

CHAPTER THIRTEEN

Quint spent a night, another full day, and another night with Two Hatchets before two young Indians rode into camp at a gallop, sliding to a stop and leaping from their paint mustangs.

Two Hatchets conferred with them a moment, then walked over to where Quint, a little apprehensive, was stirring the fire.

"Four riders, including a son of a she wolf who was a scout for Bear Coat. He's leading them here."

"Charley Tall Horse?" Quint asked, hopefully.

"That is the . . . how do you say . . . son of a bitch dog . . . who I should kill for you. He rides with the white eyes from the big ranch."

"Four is more than I want to brace—to take on—unless it's on my terms and I have the high ground. I'll ride out. Will they attack the camp?" Quint asked, not wanting to bring trouble on his friend.

"We are twenty guns strong. I'll parley with them for a while. My braves will have them surrounded. Ride on; this is not your day to die."

"Tall Horse must be a good tracker—I left little sign."

"He a son of a bitch dog but can track a hawk on the wind. Move quickly. He know I want his scalp, so he move slowly and not want to insult us. It will be midday before they get here, and I will keep them at my fire for long time. Ride swiftly, and you be able to rest easy this night."

Quint needed no more encouragement. He saddled, repacked Kit's panniers, and headed north. He planned to circle the mountain with the ragged rocks, cross the canyon with the wide stream where he'd taken care of Skunk Tobias, and head up Bald Mountain. He'd eventually cast a wide circle around the Triple R headquarters and come in from the north, a direction from which he wouldn't be expected.

When he reached the creek again, he was much higher, and it was only four feet wide. He let the animals water, refilled his canteens, checked his packsaddle, and began the climb up Bald Mountain. It was not as high as the former mountain, and after he left the firs, it was still meadow. He saw several herds of elk enjoying the tall spring grass and thought about knocking down a tender young cow but figured to get on the far side of the mountain from Two Hatchets's camp, as he knew he was being followed and didn't want to give his pursuers any more of a location than they already had.

He waited until the sun was nearing the distant horizon over the Crazy Woman Mountains before he found a place to camp near a trickle of water in a small meadow. He hobbled the mule, told Ranger to stay, grabbed his Winchester, and rode uphill through a stand of pines, then firs. He'd spotted a dozen elk from a mile away and thought he was just below them. It proved true, and when he neared the edge of the stand of fir, with a huge meadow above, he dismounted and waited.

The little herd was grazing back down the mountain coming his way. When they got within two hundred yards, just as light was failing, he ignored the big bull and a couple of smaller bulls and dropped a smaller, easier to handle barren cow with one shot. By the time he gutted her and dragged her back down to the tree line, it was getting too dark to butcher her out without a fire to light his way, and a big fire was out of the question, as the last thing he wanted was a beacon to lead his pursuers to him.

He ran his reata through the hocks of the cow, threw an end over a high branch, took a turn on the saddle horn, and hoisted her out of the reach of bears and wolves.

He let Adobe pick his way back to camp, banked a small fire against a pile of rocks, and he and Ranger enjoyed a fried elk heart, and he poured in some beans for himself. It was a feast, and he figured they'd need their strength in the morning, as he planned to move fast across Bald Mountain and down the other side.

The next morning, they feasted on the rest of the heart, then rode to where he'd hoisted the cow elk and dropped her, taking only the prime cuts, which filled the panniers.

Ten miles from the base of Bald Mountain was the Mussel-shell, and not far down river toward the Missouri Breaks he remembered an encampment and a trading post.

He was out of bacon and down to a couple of handfuls of beans, so it would be a propitious stopover. Besides, he could catch up on the news and was wondering if word of the killer who carved *C*s in his victims was getting around the territory.

He could grain the animals, catch his breath, and head east from there, which would put him only ten miles north of the Triple R headquarters . . . so long as he stayed ahead of his pursuers, or found a good place to ambush them.

Hell, they might even have a slice of ham and a few cackleberries. He could use some flapjacks as well.

It was miles from the Triple R headquarters and even miles from their west border, so he was sure he'd have no trouble, or opportunity, there.

Quint was worn to the bone by the time he started out from the base of Bald Mountain to the banks of the Musselshell. By the time he reached the muddy, slow-moving river, he'd have ridden thirty miles since sunup, half of it in rugged mountain rocks, trees, and brushand half of it across a plain cut with ravines and the occasional mud bog that would mire horse and mule to their belly.

It was another five miles downriver, north, to the trading post, if he knew where he was . . . hard to figure on the plains.

It was nearing dark when he came to the cattails lining the river, so he decided to water the stock and rest up two or three hours before he made the ride in. Besides, it would give anyone who might be at the plank bar a chance to get into their cups, and that was always an advantage for a prudent man.

After he hobbled the mule and hid the panniers and packsaddle in the reeds, he rode out letting Adobe pick his way north along the river until he could see lights from the windows of the post and from one of the two small cabins nearby. This time, he let Ranger come along, figuring the place might spare a bone or two for his faithful mutt.

The post sat on the west side of the river backed up to a fifty-foot embankment that kept it out of the prevailing winds from the northwest, and that meant a crossing, but one where a two-track road led up to one side and out of the river on the other.

When he reached the river's edge, he coaxed Ranger up into the saddle with a leap, then let Adobe find his own way across the slow-moving mud bog that was the river.

Moving at a slow walk, he carefully eyed the surroundings. A darkened barn sat behind the two-story post. The trading post itself was adobe bricks on the bottom story and log on the top. Even at two stories tall the roof was sod, and Quint could make out against the starlit night the grass and weeds growing there.

Four horses were tied at the hitching rail, no telling how many more were in the barn.

He tied Adobe at the end of the string, patting him on the neck and apologizing for leaving the latigo tight. Normally he would have loosened it, but this time he might have to make a quick exit.

With loud laughter and the plinking of a piano coming from inside, he moved from horse to horse checking their brands, a mix he didn't recognize until the last one, a big Roman-nosed bay . . . with the crooked line and verticals of Rugged Rock Ranch.

Odds were it was merely one of the hundred hands, not one of the seven . . . six now . . . he was gunning for.

CHAPTER FOURTEEN

He returned to Adobe and removed his little belly gun and four shotgun shells from a saddlebag and pocketed them, left the Winchester in its scabbard, but pulled the double-barrel coach gun from his bedroll.

Snugging his big-brimmed hat down low over his eyes, he bid

Ranger to follow and pushed his way inside.

The light was low and the room smoky and vacant. The noise came from the little room next to the trade goods where a plank bar, three tables, and a dozen chairs served as a saloon. Batwing doors separated the two rooms. He bellied up to the batwings and, from over the top of them, surveyed the room. It had been three years since he'd been in the place, and it had changed little, except for the addition of an upright piano against a far wall. A generously fleshed out soiled dove, her trade obvious because of her bare arms and exposed shoulders, sat at the piano pounding away with stubby fat fingers. Another, slender and attractive, leaned on the bar, flanked by two men. Two more sat at a table playing cards.

A man he knew to be the owner, Hiram as he recalled, worked behind the bar . . . or, to be more accurate, leaned on it from the backside. Quint remembered him as he was missing his left arm from the elbow down, probably thanks to the war.

Quint's backbone flooded with heat when he realized one of the two, the one on the left side of the girl, was a redhead with small ears. He had his right arm around her shoulders . . . his gun hand Quint noticed and couldn't help but smile. The man half turned to face the new man entering and furrowed his brows.

Quint watched him carefully as he pushed his way inside.

One of the men playing cards glanced up. "Well, hell's bells, if it ain't Sheriff Reagan."

The redheaded Irishman reacted with a dropped jaw, his small mouth forming an O, his hand dropping from the girl to rest on the six-gun at his hip. But he made no move to hoist it.

"Not sheriff any longer, just traveling by," Quint said, never taking his eyes off Shamus O'Shawnnaessy, who was now licking his lips, which Quint presumed had gone dry out of pure fear. His eyes were wide enough you could see the whites all around the pupils.

The coach gun hung at Quint's side, and as he cocked the two barrels, he said, "Young lady, I'd suggest you stand clear of that trash who's a'hangin' onto you."

"What the hell do you want, Reagan?" the Irishman sputtered.

"I want you to hoist that iron on your hip, you scum sucking excuse for a man."

The place went deadly silent, and the soiled dove slipped away; the one at the piano stopped playing.

"This ain't right," Shamus muttered. "You with a shotgun and all."

"Oh, yeah. When you beat my wife to death, was that right?"

"That was Terror did that, not me."

"You didn't stop it. And I'm sure you violated her?"

The Irishman went white.

The two men at the table rose and moved away, and the bartender, Hiram, sidled away out of the line of fire.

Ranger, at Quint's side, was growling low and ominous, the only other sound in the room.

"I ain't drawing," Shamus said, holding both hands out, palms extended, "not on no man with a scattergun."

Quint moved forward, uncocking the two barrels as he did, then swung the butt of the shotgun up between Shamus's extended arms, catching him on the chin and throwing him back across the bar. He quickly notched the hammers back again.

Ranger barked loudly, and Quint realized he was leaping to Quint's right and clearing the plank bar . . . but he was too late. The little pistol in the one-armed man's good hand roared, and Quint felt the burn in his side. He spun, cocking the coach gun again as he did so, and gave one barrel to the bartender, blowing him back and out of sight behind the bar . . . but he knew he'd hit the man solid as blood and yuck dripped down the wall behind where he'd been.

By the time Quint turned his attention back to Shamus, he'd recovered from the blow and was leveling his Colt at Quint's belly.

The second barrel roared, and half the Irishman's head left his shoulders, and he went down like a sack of grain, crashing to the floor unmoving. Quint dropped the shotgun and palmed his Smith and Wesson, panning it around the room at the three men remaining standing, but none of them had palmed a weapon, and all kept their hands in plain sight.

"Anybody else?" Quint questioned, as dust motes drifted down from the ceiling. He was answered by the vigorous shaking of three male heads and the screams from both the women. "Shut up," Quint snapped at them, and they went silent as church mice.

With his left hand, Quint fished his little folding knife out. He walked over and kicked the man he'd shot over until his remaining cheek was up, then bent and cut a large *C* in the flesh.

Then he backed toward the batwings, Ranger again at his side, still growling.

"I got some shopping to do. Don't anybody stick their nose anywhere near these doors. I'll have this scattergun reloaded and, as you can see, don't mind using it."

"You're bleeding," the thinner of the two pleasure ladies said.

"I'll live . . . long enough to carve up five more ugly cheeks with my wife's initial."

None of the men moved, but the girl stepped forward. "There's some toweling in the trading post. Can I dress that wound?"

"I'd be obliged," Quint said, backing out of the doors. "You boys go back to your whiskey. Seems it's on the house now. You can clean up the mess after I take my leave."

They didn't say a word. As soon as the doors closed behind the girl, Quint reloaded the shotgun, slamming the receiver shut hard enough that he knew the boys in the saloon could hear.

He found a bench near a potbellied stove and sat facing the batwings, the coach gun across his knees, while the girl buzzed around in the trading post. Quint, satisfied the boys in the saloon had no interest in sticking their nose in his business, leaned the shotgun against the bench and pulled his shirt out of his belt. Glancing at a wound in his side, then feeling his back and seeing that it was through and through, he sighed. A good thing, as no bullet would have to be dug out of him, and it was a small caliber.

The girl came to his side. "I'll need that knife to slice this up," she said, waving a towel at him. He produced it, watching her closely as she cut the toweling into long strips. She had to tie two together to bind a folded piece to his side, but before she did, he cautioned her.

"Get a bottle of whiskey and pour a mite on the wound, front and back."

She did so and wet the compress before she tied it in place.

"Mr. Pudquist was gonna make me a partner in the place," the girl said as she worked.

"Well, ma'am, looks like you own the whole thing now."

"You think so?" she said.

"Unless he's got a relative hereabouts. At least until someone comes along and says different," Quint said, then added quietly, "There was no reason for the damn fool to die."

"He don't like . . . didn't like . . . people causing trouble in his place. And old Shamus was a regular."

"Then he was a damn poor judge of character. I was finishing trouble, not starting it. He shoulda shot O'Shawnnaessy, not me."

"That Shamus fella owed me a dollar for a poke. He held me down until he could do it again, after he'd paid for the first one. He was a highbinder son of a whore with breath like the floor of a chicken coop."

"Well, ma'am, you at least are a good judge of character. Were I you, I'd get in there and dig a dollar plus a good tip out of his pockets before those other owlhoots clean him out."

"Good idea," she said and spun on her heels.

"Thanks for the nursing," Quint said and headed for the door. He yelled over his shoulder, "Remember, I see a face, I blow it to hell."

Chapter Fifteen

He was glad he'd left Adobe tightly saddled as he lifted himself aboard with a wince and a moan. Damn if his side wasn't beginning to hurt something awful.

Gigging the big horse into a lope, he almost took a dive from the saddle into the Musselshell as Adobe leaped into the water, then lunged to the other side. Ranger had to swim, and as the big horse pounded back toward where Kit was hobbled, Quint had to hang on and let the horse have his head.

He managed to remove the hobbles from Kit and get him repacked, if badly, and since he couldn't backtrack as he had pursuers on that trail, he made a wide northerly circle leaving the riverside trail but heading north toward the Missouri Breaks. He'd had to lead the big horse over to a downed cottonwood and climb up on the log to get in the saddle.

After an hour, he passed out in the saddle, lying across the horse's neck and hanging on out of pure instinct. Luckily Kit and Ranger followed Adobe's lead.

He awoke, feverish, lying by the trail. The dog was nestled against his side, Kit was dragging his lead rope and Adobe his reins, but they were grazing nearby as the morning sun washed the sky lemon yellow and streaming under a high solid overcast. To add insult to injury, it started to rain.

His side was soaked in blood, but the wound seemed to have stopped leaking.

Having no idea how much blood he'd lost, he managed to sit up and rebind the toweling, now brown with dried blood.

Nauseated, he pulled himself to his feet, and, deciding he couldn't mount, tied Kit's lead rope to his packsaddle and looped Adobe's reins over his neck, then stumbled off to the north. Walking, stumbling, away from his pursuers. Away from the mess he'd left at the Musselshell Trading Post.

Then the rain began to pound. A grove of cottonwood offered some shelter, and a downfall of a large cottonwood tree crossed by another became a lifesaver as he pulled a couple of pack canvases from the panniers and made a makeshift tent across cottonwood branches with one and rolled up in the other on a slope that drained the rainfall away. He was able to keep relatively dry in the cocoon of the pack canvas.

He awoke with the river licking at his feet.

It was still raining, and the river would continue to rise, so he had to move. Nauseated, dizzy, and now in the open and wet and cold to the bone, he stumbled up a low rise and saw a rising sandstone cliff in the distance. Getting closer, he realized that some deep wind caves were carved into the sandstone face, and he managed to work his way through cattails, then river willow, then cottonwoods until he reached the bank. With some effort and afraid he would pass out, he managed to get deep enough in a wind cave to get out of the rain. Ranger never left his side.

He awoke again, the rain still falling but gently, and managed to exit the cave and find the animals and drop their saddles and headstalls but didn't have the strength to hobble them. He stumbled back to the cave with a frying pan, bedroll, some jerky, and his canteens all while dragging a rotten cottonwood branch.

With a last effort, he pinned one of the canvas pack covers across the mouth of the shallow cave with his hunting knife to one corner and his folding knife the other. Then, lying prone, he busted up the rotten log and after carefully shaving bark and limbs to fine tinder got a fire going. He fixed a watery jerky soup, ate a frying pan full, then managed to get his trousers and shirt off and paste them against the cave wall to dry.

When he again awoke, he had no idea how long he'd slept. But it was dark outside.

Feeling less nauseated but now feverish, he built another fire and cooked another batch of soup.

He managed to get outside and relieve himself and was pleased to see Adobe and Kit grazing nearby. Stumbling back to his bed, he again dropped into a deep slumber.

The next time he awoke, it was light, so he again managed to crawl to his feet and get outside. Meadowlarks and yellow-winged blackbirds were singing and squawking happily. The sun was so bright it hurt his eyes and directly overhead, so it was noon . . . maybe later. Sunshine was the good news; the bad was his animals were nowhere in sight. It was the first time Ranger had been gone; then he realized he'd fed himself but not the dog. He was likely hunting a rabbit or gopher.

He couldn't blame the dog for hunting a meal, nor the horse and mule for wandering wherever good grass took them.

Even with a feverish mind he knew he couldn't stay where he was. He would run out of food and suspected his wound would go green if not treated by someone who knew what they were doing. He had to move, no matter how tough it might be.

The closest place was the Musselshell Trading Post, but he couldn't go there. They had probably sent for the law. The second closest was the Triple R headquarters, where he was damn sure a rope and high limb or barn beam and fancy hangman's dance awaited.

And how the hell would he get to either on shank's mare.

He had to find his animals. Luckily, his wound was puckered and ugly but not bleeding. He pulled his knives and stumbled down to the willows and worked long and hard cutting one that would serve as a walking stick. He pulled his reata from its saddle tie, hoping he'd have use for it, and hung it from a shoulder. Then he hobbled along like a ninety-year-old man, wearing no shirt and enjoying the sun on his back even though he was hot to the touch already. After what seemed an eternity, but looking back was only a quarter mile, he pulled up to rest and reconnoiter.

On a ridge a quarter mile distant, he saw the dark outline of two four-footed animals backlit by a beautiful blue sky. Getting closer, even with his vision blurred, he knew it was Kit and Adobe, as the critters didn't run from a stumblebum of a man.

The big horse not only didn't run it walked to meet him.

He tied a Spanish hackamore in the reata and adjusted it to fit Adobe, then led him to a rock and managed to get mounted bareback. The horse readily moved back to where his tack rested in the mud. It took most of two hours, but he got both horse and mule saddled and packed. He had to dump the heavy load of meat from his panniers in order to heft them up to the packsaddle, but it was just as well as he didn't have the strength to build a fire, and a fire large enough to smoke meat would likely attract the varmints who followed.

When he managed to get mounted, he gave light heels to the horse and dozed as he backtracked the way they'd come. Soon he realized that Ranger had joined up with them. That, too, made him smile.

He was nearing the trading post he figured, so he reined away and up to the top of a ridge that looked down on the river and soon on the trading post complex on its far side.

He reined up in a copse of alders and watched the buildings for a while. Now there were at least eight horses at the hitching rail. While he watched, four men left the place and mounted up and headed out downriver. One of them had long braids and was dressed in buckskin . . . and Quint wished he had the strength and resolve to pull his Winchester and drop the Indian, Tall Horse.

Even feverish Quint smiled, as with luck they were following his trail, and he knew the rain would make it very, very difficult. If the Blackfoot tracker could read through the washout and the puddles, he was more than merely an excellent tracker, he was part devil.

It was a hard, hard day's ride with him seeming to come in and out of consciousness. Then he saw country he recognized and knew that Two Hatchets's camp was somewhere nearby.

He was quietly elated, until he came upon some cold campfires and the tracks of travois leading off downhill; but downhill to the north, the way he'd come. And the way his pursuers would likely be following him if they found any trail at all to follow.

He'd have to look for help somewhere else.

Not knowing how far he'd ridden, but knowing he'd stopped at least twice to spend the night, he again awoke flat on his back. The animals grazed nearby; Ranger lay at his side. He was hallucinating, he recognized, as he saw Consuela and his long-dead parents, who were smiling at him.

Then he saw the boy . . . what was his name? Tommy, that was it, and the boy was calling his name. Was he a hallucination?

"Mr. Reagan. Mr. Reagan, we got to get you back to the cabin. Can you get up?"

Then he realized the hallucination was shaking him awake.

CHAPTER SIXTEEN

"Tommy," Quint managed.

"Yes, sir. You're hurt bad and hot as Hades. A pack of wolves was watchin' you when I rode up. We got to get you back to Ma."

Then the boy was dragging him up, helping him stand, then helping him up into the saddle. And he was a clever boy. He took one of the packsaddle covers and slit it into strips and tied Quint's legs to the latigo rings, and his wrists together under the horse's neck so it would be all but impossible for him to fall off the animal. He even padded the saddle horn with the rest of the pack cover.

Then he walked, leading Adobe.

Again, Quint had no idea how much time passed, but this time when he awoke, there was a cold, wet compress on his forehead, and Sarah McLaughton was bending over him. At first, he wondered if he was dead and she was an angel, then he chuckled to himself as it would more likely be Beelzebub poking at him.

"Thank God," she said, "you've regained consciousness."

"Oh," Quint managed.

" 'Oh' is right. However, this might have been easier had you been out."

"What might?" he questioned.

"I've got to cut some bad flesh out of your wound. A bullet hole, I presume."

"Yes, ma'am. You do what needs doing."

"It's not going to be enjoyable, Mr. Reagan."

"The last few days have not been, ma'am. You do what needs doing. That's not the first bullet hole in this old hide of mine."

"I'm going to tie your hands together under the cot and tie

your legs down. I don't want you slapping me away while I'm doing delicate work."

". . . whatever needs doing," he managed then, thankfully, passed out again.

He awoke with Tommy untying his wrists, then watched as he untied his legs. The boy was startled when he looked over and saw Quint watching him.

"Ma, he's awake," the boy called over his shoulder.

In seconds the woman, looking even more like an angel to Quint, was at the bedside.

"You get it cleaned up?" Quint asked.

"I pray enough so," she said. "I packed it, but you'll forever have a deep indentation on the back side. The front side should heal fine. Can you take a little broth?"

He hesitated before he said it, but then, "It smells like death in here."

"That's the stench of green flesh, Mr. Reagan. Your own."

"Sorry to bring that into your home. My fever seems to be down?"

"I thought you were going to burst into flame there for a while. Yes, it's way down. Now, take some soup."

"Yes, ma'am."

Then he realized she'd called him by his real name and wondered. While she was spooning it in, she kept up a conversation. "Paddy O'Brady, Braddick's travelling baker and cook, was by here yesterday and told me some of what Hong, Braddick's in-house cook, told him . . ."

Quint's brow furrowed, but as soon as he opened his mouth, she shoved another spoonful of soup in.

"I know who you are and about your wife, Mr. Reagan . . . at least as much as Hong picked up listening in on everything around the Triple R. I understand you and what you're doing. And I understand why you lied to us about who you were. I don't approve of your actions but understand them. I wouldn't have understood before my husband was murdered. And I sure don't approve of Braddick and how he runs his outfit . . . or his life. So you're safe here, so long as it doesn't endanger my son. You understand?"

Quint nodded, and she barely took a breath.

"Not all Triple R riders are evil, but those close to Braddick are, sure as hell is hot. Paddy's a fine man, and so are most of the riders."

Quint kept his jaw clamped until she pulled the next spoonful back.

Then he spoke up, low and slow. "Ma'am, I have no bone to pick with anyone except those six who molested and murdered my wife, and the man who sent them there."

"Then there's been enough said about it. You can stay here until you're well enough to ride. Then I want you to pack up and ship out. And if I were you, I'd ship out on a clipper for the South Seas and get the hell away from this evil place."

Quint was silent for a long while, then said in all sincerity, "It's not the place, Mrs. McLaughton. It's the men. A place is only as good or evil as the folks who hang out there. This place has plenty of good to go 'round for all of us . . . so long as we don't pollute it with man's rotten work."

She sighed deeply. "We got stuck here, Mr. Reagan—"

"Quint, if you would, please."

"Then Quint, and I'm Sarah. Anyway, we got stuck here under the worst of circumstances. Then Brad Braddick showed us what we thought was a kindness, but then he turned out to be evil as Satan himself. So, it's hard for me to see the beauty in this godforsaken country."

Again Quint was quiet for a while, then he said, "Well, Sarah, I hope to be able to help you as you've helped me . . . and that would be to get you to anywhere you'd like to go."

"First, we've got to get you well, and it seems you have some other things requiring your attention. Things, by the way, I don't want my son privy to . . . understand?"

"Yes, ma'am."

"If you've had enough soup, you should sleep and heal."

"Yes, ma'am . . . Sarah."

She smiled tightly and moved away from his cot.

As he lay trying to get back to sleep, it came to him that he was in no condition for a face-to-face fight with anyone and wouldn't be for a while, so now it was time to put his well-learned marksmanship skills to work. They were now hunting him, so it would soon be time for the hunted to become the hunter.

Chapter Seventeen

The foreman of the Triple R was not above having a drink or visiting the others and commiserating over the two dead bodies in the back room, one of which was a cohort of his. Of course, they were commiserating with whiskey belonging to the other dead soul, over the objections of a soiled dove who now claimed to own the place.

After spending a few hours at the trading post, pleasuring the ladies and getting their fill of whiskey and vittles, the Triple R boys rode on in pursuit.

Spike Howard, Torrance "Terror" Oliver, young Tony Balducci, and Charley Tall Horse had found where Quint had holed up, more from luck than good tracking.

It seems Reagan had lightened his packs by dumping a load of fresh meat, which had attracted a bevy of turkey vultures and magpies. Tall Horse had spotted them and, knowing that Reagan had been shot by the proprietor of the Musselshell Trading Post, hoped to find the attraction was Reagan's rotting body, but it was not. Yet there was plenty of sign that Reagan had holed up in a nearby wind cave, and sign of his leaving and heading back south.

Spike wondered if they hadn't passed near him as they came north along the river. When they reached the base of Bald Mountain, Tall Horse, who'd ridden on ahead, was waiting for them.

"He is sick, or injured badly," Tall Horse said, a mouthful for the normally taciturn Indian.

"How do you know that?" Spike asked, then wondered why he bothered to question the tracker, who always proved himself.

"See how horse wanders—he stops to munch grass. Rider is still in saddle but not in control."

"Good," Spike snapped, then turned back to Balducci and Oliver. "Keep an eye out. He's probably down in the brush somewhere along the trail . . . dead with any luck."

Both the men nodded at him.

But they rode on seeing nothing and finally camping at the spot where the Sioux had been.

Quint awoke with the sun, feeling much better. Still weak, but his fever seemed to have broken.

Sarah was already in front of the fire, stirring a generous pot of oats. He lay quietly, watching her, realizing that he was enjoying watching a fine-looking woman at work. The front door banged shut, making him jump, then wince.

Tommy walked over and smiled at him. "I give your animals some grain. That's a—"

"You gave his animals some grain," his mother corrected.

"I gave your animals some grain. That's a fine dog you got there, Mr. Reagan."

"He's been a faithful friend," Quint said. "You can take him hunting with you, if you'd like."

Sarah stopped her stirring. "Tommy, you leave that dog here.

I like having a watchdog, and God only knows who's tracking Mr. Reagan."

"Quint," Quint corrected.

"Quint," she repeated and went back to stirring.

In moments she headed his way, a bowl in one hand and a little mug in the other.

She motioned with the mug. "Honey."

"The Good Lord knows I need sweetening up," Quint said, with a smile. Then he turned serious. "Put that on the table, please. I'm getting up."

"Hogwash," she snapped.

"No, ma'am." He was adamant. "I'm getting up."

She eyed him, shook her head, then turned and took the three steps to the table and arranged the bowl, the mug, and a spoon. He glanced to the floor behind the cot and was pleased to see all his firearms nicely placed there, with boxes of ammunition beside each piece.

That was kind of her, if a little reckless, as she really had no idea what kind of a fella he was.

Quint carefully swung his legs to the side of the cot and tried to sit up, grimaced, then called out to Tommy. "Hey, boy, give an old man a little help here." He extended a hand, and Tommy gave him a pull and got him upright, then to his feet. Tommy let him lean on a shoulder as they shuffled to the table. Quint plopped down, again wincing.

"You'll pardon me saying so, Quint," Sarah said, her lips tight, "but you're a damn fool."

"Ma!" Tommy exclaimed, never before hearing his mother use any kind of a swear word.

"Your ma is right, Tommy. I'm six kinds of a damn fool." He gave Sarah a smile, then again got serious. "I'll be riding out after this fine breakfast."

"Over my dead body," Sarah snapped. "You'll kill yourself,

trying to ride."

"You were right about me being tracked, and I don't intend to make trouble for you."

"Tommy is going to move your horse and mule down to a meadow he knows a mile or so away, and he'll brush out the tracks for a couple of hundred yards from the house. If they come, you can hide in the root cellar. You need a few more days."

"Then tomorrow."

"We'll see," she said, but he could tell she doubted if he'd be ready tomorrow or even the day after.

"Thank you for breakfast," he said, changing the subject.

"Thank you for the coffee," she said, with a smile, walking over with a pot and cup and pouring him one. "Tommy found it in your pack, and we were out. And I miss my coffee."

"Glad I could do something," he said, then busied himself with the oats and honey.

Later in the day, after sleeping a while, he was sitting up in the cot when he heard Ranger begin to bark.

Chapter Eighteen

Sarah moved quickly to the only window in the soddy, a two-foot square with four one-foot-square glass panes. She looked for only a second, then turned back.

"The root cellar," she said.

He moved more quickly than he might have thought possible, snatching up his Russian in its holster and cartridge lined belt, and the shotgun.

The root cellar was dug into the hillside, the two-foot-wide by five-foot-tall entrance covered with a tall pie safe. He helped her swing it aside, and she talked as they did so.

"There's four of them. They are surrounding the place. That

foreman, Spike, looks to be coming to the door. Make no sound."

He helped from the inside, pulling the pie safe back in place, just as there was a rap on the door.

"Why, if it isn't Mr. Howard," he heard her say.

"One and the same," he replied, his voice deep and resonant. "You gonna invite me in?"

"I'm alone here, Mr. Howard. It wouldn't be proper."

"Tony," he heard the foreman yell. "Come on over here and chaperone."

"Sir?" the voice was far away.

"Get in here!"

"What makes you think," she stammered, "that two men and one lone woman is proper?"

"Proper or not, we're gonna have a look-see around."

"Does Mr. Braddick know how you act? I'm a guest of his, you know."

"You take it up with him the next time you sleep at his house," Spike said, his voice contemptuous.

Quint felt his jaw tighten and the heat crawl up his neck. He suddenly felt possessive of Mrs. McLaughton. But he was in no shape to take on four armed men. It was dark as a foot up a bull's butt in the root cellar, which was only five feet wide and twice as deep. But he didn't need light to strap on the Russian.

"Then," she said, "do what you must, then get out."

"Where's your boy?" Spike said, and Quint could hear them moving about on the hard clay surface of the floors, only partly covered with rugs.

"He's doing his job . . . hunting."

There was a long silence, then Quint heard the cot slide aside, and suddenly wished he had gathered up all his weapons.

"You didn't have no Winchester," Spike said.

"Tommy found them, out on the prairie, on a dead man."

There was another long silence. Then Spike asked, "He didn't find no scattergun?"

"Scattergun?" she asked, innocently.

"Shotgun . . . you know, a side by side with two barrels."

"Yes, he did; he's got it with him."

"You don't hunt wolves with no shotgun," Spike snapped.

"He's hunting sage hens for meat."

"Where's this dead man?"

"We buried him."

"Where?"

"Out on the prairie."

"God damn it, woman, where out on the prairie?"

"Don't you curse at me, Spike Howard. I don't know . . . a few miles out there." Quint presumed she was pointing. Then it seemed she tried to change the subject.

"Young Tony."

"Yes'm."

"I heard some terrible things happened over on the Yellowstone. Were you part of that?"

"Ma'am?"

"Were you part of molesting that woman?"

"How the hell . . ." Spike managed.

"No, ma'am," Tony said. "I stayed outside. It made me sick to my stomach."

"Shut up, Balducci," Spike said. "And you keep your mouth shut, woman, or you'll get the same."

Again, there was a long silence, then Spike challenged, "They was a root cellar on this place. I hear'd Hong brought you a sack of potatoes and turnips and carrots. Where is it?"

"Outside, about fifty feet that way. It's an old mine shaft."

"Tony, you watch her."

"Yes, sir."

Quint could hear footfalls, then the door open and close.

"Give me a hand, here, Tony," Sarah said.

He presumed Sarah knew that Spike would return, ready for bear when he found no root cellar in the bank outside, and Quint knew she was giving him the best chance she could.

"Help me," she repeated.

"What's back there," Tony asked.

Quint stood at the ready as the pie safe slid aside.

Young Tony's eyes flared, and his mouth dropped open.

"Please," Sarah said, "don't kill him; he's hardly more than a child."

The boy was heeled and backpedaled, his hand going for the revolver at his side.

Quint stepped forward and drove the butt of the shotgun into the boy's gut, and he doubled, then he brought the stock across the boy's head before he could straighten. Tony went to his knees, and Quint kicked him hard in the stomach. He folded into a fetal position, gasping for breath.

Grabbing the boy's revolver, already half out of his holster, Quint shoved him aside and stuffed the revolver in his belt.

"You got any rope?" Quint asked.

She shook her head. "It's out in the animal lean-to."

Quint put both barrels under the boy's chin and spoke loud enough to be heard over his wheezing. "You want to see another day, you crawl over to that corner and keep your mouth shut. Understand?"

The boy managed to shake his head as he moved away.

Then Quint turned to the woman. "Our only chance is if I kill them all."

"Oh, God, no. Not here."

"No choice. You get out of harm's way . . . in the root cellar."

She hesitated.

"Now," he demanded, and she ran for the darkness.

"Stay out of the line of fire," Quint snapped, then heard the sound of footfalls outside, a man moving fast.

He was sure he'd get one of them, but there were two more outside, and one of them, Terror Oliver, was a known shooter. A man it was rumored had killed a half-dozen men in saloon and range war shootouts. And Spike Howard carried his own reputation.

And, of course, there was the half-black, half-Indian Tall Horse.

CHAPTER NINETEEN

Quint questioned how smart Spike Howard was when he threw the door aside in anger and still had his weapon holstered. His eyes widened when he saw Quint standing there, shotgun in hand and cocked.

"Jesus, Mother, and Mary," Spike stammered.

"They won't help you now," Quint said as Spike backpedaled, reaching for the revolver at his side. The shotgun roared as Quint fired a single barrel in the small soddy, and every piece of dust that might have come down in the next year was jarred loose and rained a dust storm.

Spike threw both hands up and windmilled backward, then went to his back as blood mushroomed over his chest. His eyes were wide and unmoving by the time he gasped only one time.

Quint moved forward as quickly as he could and flattened his back against the front wall of the cabin and waited. He heard footfalls, running coming down each side but both out of his line of sight.

It was Terror Oliver who rounded a corner first, his revolver in hand, his eyes on Howard unmoving on the ground.

Quint fired a little quickly, taking him in a shoulder, but it was his gun-hand shoulder, and he dropped his weapon as he made a three-sixty and fell to his side. He cried out like a coyote trying to find a mate.

But Quint didn't take time to finish him off, as he knew the Indian was coming.

He palmed his Smith and Wesson and, as soon as Tall Horse made the corner, fired.

The big Indian oofed loudly and spun out of sight behind the cabin. Quint knew he was hit but had no idea how bad; then he heard footfalls going away at a run.

By the time Quint reached the corner of the soddy, Tall Horse was mounted and beating his heels into a paint horse's ribs.

Quint fired all five remaining shots, but the Indian was lying low across the horse's withers and not much of a target, fast moving at more than a hundred feet. He disappeared over the ridge the cabin was dug into.

"Damn the flies," Quint mumbled and started back toward the house.

"You bastard," Terror Oliver said, his revolver now in his left hand.

And Quint's was empty.

Terror was bleeding out but seemed to have enough left. From only twenty feet away, he leveled his six-shooter on Quint's middle.

Only then did Quint remember the boy's revolver, shoved into his belt, and he reached for it but knew he'd be too late.

A shot roared out, and Quint presumed he'd soon meet his maker, but the shot had come from inside the soddy, and Terror rolled to the side, dropping his weapon.

Sarah McLaughton stepped into the doorway, Quint's smoking Winchester in hand.

Quint smiled at her. "All that, and a fine oatmeal cook as well."

But she didn't see the humor and replied with a tight jaw, "I took no pleasure in that, but it seemed it had to be done. Please don't tell Tommy."

Quint nodded, then in the distance, he saw a rider coming at a dead gallop. He reached over and took the Winchester out of Sarah's hands and levered in another shell.

"That's Tommy," Sarah said, and Quint lowered the rifle's muzzle.

Tommy reached the yard, slid his horse to a stop, and leapt from the saddle, rifle in hand. "You okay, Ma? I heard the shooting."

"I'm fine."

Tommy eyed the two men on the ground. "Damn, they don't look so good."

"They came after Mr. Reagan. He had no choice."

For the first time, Quint eyed the rifle Braddick had loaned the boy to hunt wolves. A Sharps.

"45-90?" Quint asked.

"45-70," the boy answered, "but she'll reach right out there."

Quint reached for it and handed the boy the Winchester in the same movement. Tommy handed him the weapon.

"How many shells you got?" Quint asked.

"A half dozen left. I got to reload a dozen brass I got."

"Give me them, please," Quint said.

"I gotta use that rifle for my job of work."

"You'll get it back," Quint said, then said a little more strongly, "Hand them over."

"Give them to him, Tommy," Sarah said.

The boy dug into both pants' pockets and produced three shells out of each.

"How long you been riding that horse hard?" Quint asked.

"Only a half mile or so. I was on my way home."

"Help me into the saddle." He slipped the long thirty-two-inch barrel into a saddle scabbard, and the boy got behind him and shoved him up in the saddle.

"That'll kill you," Sarah said, tears beginning to make her eyes shine.

"And if that Indian reaches the headquarters, they'll be coming back here with two dozen riders, and that'll kill me for sure . . . and maybe you and the boy as well." Then he turned to the boy. "Tommy, I hate to leave you with this mess, and as far as I'm concerned you can tie a line to this trash in your yard and drag it out to the desert for the coyotes and skunks."

"Tommy and the boy inside will bury them," Sarah said.

She hesitated for a moment, then added, "Go with God, Quint Reagan. But come back."

"I intend to, Sarah McLaughton. The Indian will slow down. I think he's hit, and he'd better not let me get within a half mile of him. You tell that boy in the house that you saved his hide, as he was on my list. He's to help you pack and get you where you want to go. And if he's smart, he'll keep on going."

"Then you'll come back?" she asked, the tears now streaking her cheeks.

"I've got business at Triple R headquarters; then I'll come back. No matter my return or not, you pack what you can get on my mule, you take my weapons with my compliments, and if I'm not back in three days, you light out for Bozeman or wherever you need to go. You tell that kid if he doesn't get you where you want to go, he's going back on my list. You'll find three thousand dollars in gold coin sewed into the bottom of Kit's packsaddle. That'll get you a new start."

"I've never seen that much money. I can't—" she started to say.

"Yes, you can. You saved my hide twice, so, yes, you can."

He gigged the roan horse into an easy lope, and, although his side pained him, he was driven and meant to complete the job he'd set out to do.

CHAPTER TWENTY

Now he was the tracker. And it was easy, as there was not only a clear set of hoofprints, at a gallop for a mile or so then at a walk, but also the occasional dollop of blood. It was too much for a man to lose, so Quint had to believe he'd hit the paint horse.

He moved at a steady pace, walking a quarter mile, then into a lope for somewhat more than that.

The sun was about to touch the horizon to the west, so he knew he'd likely not catch up to Tall Horse before darkness overtook him. But he had time; it was Tall Horse's time that was limited.

He spent the night in a cold camp, the roan watered by a vernal pool, now full from the last rain. He still was a long way from right but had little trouble saddling the horse with the first hint of light. And, by the time the sun topped the horizon, he was two miles down the trail, letting the animal have his head.

When it was full light, he realized he'd lost the track, so he ranged back and forth, losing time but not so much as he would have if he had no track to follow.

He had yet to pick up the Indian's track again when he topped a low rise and spotted a rider not more than a half mile ahead, on a paint horse. He gigged the roan into a lope and gained a quarter mile before the Indian, to his surprise, spotted him and reined up.

Quint slowed to a walk and watched the big man pull a long gun from his saddle scabbard, walk to a pile of rocks, and settle down to wait.

At three hundred yards, Quint reined up and dismounted, pulling the Sharps from the saddle scabbard.

A shot rang out, and dust kicked up ten feet to Quint's right as he walked to a small mound, probably a badger hole.

As he settled down another shot rang out, and this time the

shell plowed into the ground only five feet to his right.

He took his time, hunkering down into a prone position, using the mound. He'd never fired this Sharps but was completely familiar with the double-set trigger and the vernier long-range sights. He set the sight at three hundred yards as another shell kicked up dirt and rocks, this time splattering the side of his face with shards. He ignored it.

Taking a deep breath, he centered what he could see of Tall Horse in the vernier, released the back trigger setting the front, and gently squeezed the forward one.

The big rifle bucked in his hands.

Even at the distance, he could see Tall Horse's head explode in a shower of bone and gore.

He dug another shell out of his pocket, dropped the block on the Sharps and extracted the brass, and reloaded. The formerly familiar weapon felt good in his hands.

There was no hurry, so Quint rolled to his back and rubbed his shoulder where the big rifle had made an indentation.

He rested, as it had been a long fourteen hours since he'd ridden away from Sarah's house. Finally, he rose, walked to the roan, and replaced the Sharps in its saddle scabbard. When he came up to the body, he was not surprised that there was no movement.

The Indian's shoulder was bullet creased and had been bleeding.

Removing his hunting knife he knelt by the man and with two deft cuts removed his long braids. His hat had been blown five feet away, and Quint fetched it. He put two slices in the very broad-brimmed, easily recognized felt and ran the braids through the slits so they'd hang at his back like the Indian's had.

Then he stripped the man down, removing his buckskins, leaving his body for the critters.

He slowly undressed, packing his clothes in the roan's saddlebags. The Indian's paint was now grazing a hundred yards away, and Quint walked over. He smiled as the horse was well trained and didn't move away on his approach. A gouge was cut through the skin on the paint's rump, and he was streaked with his own blood but not badly injured. He led the animal back, used one of the rocks to help himself remount the roan, then rode away leading the paint, toward the Triple R headquarters.

Like the reversed collar had done, he hoped his current disguise would get him close to the last man on his list—Brad Braddick.

CHAPTER TWENTY-ONE

Part of the Triple R ranch headquarters was two story and part one. Brad Braddick lived there alone, never having taken a wife. The only other residents of the big house were the houseboy, Choo, and Hong and his wife. Quint had long heard about the rather elegant house, as it was the talk of the Judith Basin and surrounding towns and had been for many years. Three guest rooms graced the upper story, Quint knew, and may or may not have been occupied.

The roundup was underway and gathering pens were a half mile from the house and its compound, which included a large hay barn, a birthing barn, a milking barn, a blacksmith and tack shop, and a horse barn. Braddick was industrious and kept a small dairy and made cheese and butter, which were distributed to his line camps and sold as far away as Bozeman, Helena, and Fort Benton. They were even sold in bulk to the side-wheelers plying the Missouri and probably ended up as far away as St. Louis.

A thousand cattle were gathered in the pens, and more were being driven there. But all were so distant that no one could make the paint rider's features. One man, only two hundred yards from Quint, even waved. Quint extended his hand, palm out, Indian fashion, and the man went back to his work, hazing a couple of cows and calves back toward the pens.

Quint had staked the roan out in a meadow where he could reach a trickle of water, not more than two miles from the headquarters, and mounted the paint. In buckskins and with the tall brimmed hat Tall Horse wore, and his braids hanging down behind, a man would have to be close to see it was not the half-Negro, half-Indian tracker that had been on Braddick's payroll since he had worked as a scout for Bear Coat, as General Miles was called by the tribes.

Reining the paint around to the back of the house, he passed the blacksmith and tack shop where a man was shoeing a horse, and another worked at a draw-down table repairing a saddle. Neither paid him much attention, and he didn't give them as much as a glance.

He reined up at a hitching rail and approached the house between two large maple trees that Braddick must have imported years ago, as they were each eighteen inches in diameter and forty feet tall.

Quint carried the Sharps, had the Russian on his hip, and had one of the owlhoot's revolvers in his belt.

When he pushed the door in and stepped inside, Hong and his wife were busy at a table covered with flour. The woman glanced up but returned her eyes to her work. Hong looked up and stopped short, his eyes going wide, his mouth dropping open.

"You not Tall Horse," he said.

Quint nodded, removed the hat and braids with one hand, and let it fall to the floor while he panned the two cooks with the muzzle of the big Sharps.

"No, sir, I'm not. I'm a heathen white devil, and they'll be taking your body back to China to visit your ancestors unless you take your lady and run for one of those barns."

"I tell the mister you here," he said, brushing the flour off his hands, then wiping them on the apron he wore.

"No, you will not. You will take your woman and run for a barn. You understand?"

Hong nodded rapidly, his own queue rivaling the length of the Tall Horse braids, bouncing off his back as he grabbed the wrist of his wife and headed for the door.

Quint waited until he could see Hong and his wife well away from the house, then worked his way into a large dining room with a table that would easily seat twelve, then into a great room with a fireplace one could cook a good-sized pig in if it had a spit, then across to a closed paneled door.

A voice rang out from inside. "Hong, that you? Bring me another cup of that mud you call coffee."

Quint pushed the door open. Braddick sat at a large desk, his head down, *pince-nez* glasses perched on his nose as he studied a journal. One wall of the large office was shelves and a huge library, and between it and the boss's desk and chairs was a billiard table with carved legs and lion's feet.

Quint stood in the doorway until Braddick glanced up, then paled and pushed back from the desk, his back to a pair of large windows each with three-dozen panes.

"Who the hell are you?" Braddick managed.

"You know who the hell I am and why the hell I'm here," Quint said, a crooked smile, or smirk, on his face.

"I didn't have nothing to do—"

"A fella probably shouldn't lie with what might be his last breath," Quint said.

Braddick was silent for a moment. Quint did not have the Sharps trained on the man. In fact, the muzzle was almost pointing at the Oriental carpet covering the polished wood floor.

Braddick spoke up. "You think I had something to do with

what happened to your wife?"

Quint was in no hurry, as he wanted the fat son of a bitch to sweat, to suffer as Consuela had done.

Finally, Quint replied. "You want me to believe you had nothing to do with that?"

"Yes. Those men worked for the Triple R, but they were supposed to go into Big Horn and pick up supplies."

Quint couldn't help but laugh. Then he parried, "So, you want me to believe that men without a buckboard were going after supplies? You know, Braddick, you shouldn't underestimate folks, like thinking a man couldn't ride up to your back door and stick a Sharps up your ass to blow your goddamned ugly head off."

Braddick blanched even whiter but was inching back toward his desk. Quint smiled as the man tried to slide open a side desk drawer while he distracted his adversary.

"Yes, I want to buy your place. In fact, you can leave here with your price, in gold coin."

While he spoke, he slid the drawer open wider at the same time as Quint cocked the Sharps.

Braddick had hardly gotten the revolver out of the drawer when the five hundred-grain bullet from the Sharps blew him back against one of the windows. It shattered several panes, but the mullions didn't give way and instead sprang him back to sprawl over his desktop. The big bullet had caught him flush in the sternum and blown a chunk the size of a fist out of the middle of his back.

It was over . . . almost.

It would have been totally over, but he'd made a promise to a woman and her son to see her safely off the Triple R, and to wherever she wanted to be.

And Quint knew he had to do it soon, as he was now on the wrong side of the law. Having killed a man who was a friend of governors, senators, and bankers, he knew that posters would be spread far and wide over the West.

As he moved back through the house, he paused in the kitchen, noting that Hong's stove was red hot, awaiting the bread half kneaded on the table.

He walked to a pantry and found a large keg of coal oil, unstoppered it, and walked back through the kitchen, into the dining room, and into the living room until the keg was drained. He went back to the stove, opened the firebox, and used a large wooden spoon from the table to fling glowing coals out onto the spilled oil. It lit, and tongues of flame arose as it tracked the path into the rest of the house.

As he headed for the paint horse, the blacksmith and saddle maker were running toward the house. He stopped them with a wave of the Sharps.

"I got no bone to pick with you. Your boss is a dead man, killed by a man avenging his wife, who was murdered and violated at his order. You two head back to your business. There's nothing you can do now but watch this evil burn."

Both the men backed away, arms extended, palms out. Neither was armed, and it seemed neither was prepared to die.

Quint didn't notice the pain in his side as he mounted, gigged the paint, and loped away. Two miles from the house, with it now totally involved in flame and smoke billowing a thousand feet in the air, Quint dismounted, changed his clothes, left the buckskins in a heap, and rode out on the roan.

He had one more job of work to worry about.

Chapter Twenty-Two

It took him two full days, even riding one of the horses and trading off to the other, to get back to the soddy, and he was pleased to see it empty. He'd had to take two six-hour breaks to sleep, as his body was still not up to sleepless nights on horseback.

Their trail led off to the southwest, but he needed some rest, so he slept one night in the soddy, on the cot where Sarah McLaughton had probably saved his life.

He rose with the sun, fried himself some of the potatoes left in the root cellar, then set out on the trail of the young Tony Balducci, Sarah McLaughton, and her son, Tommy.

He was healing, feeling better every day, maybe every hour, so he pushed hard. It was the second night before he sat on a hill overlooking Bozeman City, a booming mining town of over two hundred population on the banks of Bozeman Creek. Both coal and gold-silver mines spotted the hills around the town.

Because he had been a sheriff in Big Horn, two hundred miles to the east, he knew the sheriff who maintained an office in Bozeman, and the sheriff knew him. But Quint doubted if news of his recent activities had reached the city as of yet. He hoped not. He had to make sure Sarah McLaughton and son were safe and settled.

So he boldly gigged the roan down the hill. With almost seventy buildings, the town was substantial for Montana. Like most frontier mining towns, the primary commercial establishment was saloons, and Bozeman City already boasted six, as well as a brewery that served its product on site in a fairly substantial building constructed over the creek to take advantage of the cold, clear mountain runoff.

He rode straight to what seemed to be the busiest saloon on the muddy main street and reined up at a hitching rail. Sounds of a fiddle and violin poured out of the Grizzly's Lament, as the sign announced.

Two burly miners moved out of the batwing doors as Quint paused and surveyed the place. Even though he was sure news of the big fire and killing at the Triple R had yet to reach Bozeman, he didn't want to risk running into the law.

But he saw no familiar faces. He pushed his way inside and up to the bar, leaning the Sharps up beneath him.

"You got a cold beer?" he asked the man in a black vest with bright-red garters on his shirtsleeves.

"I got one, pilgrim, if you got the dime."

In moments he was sipping the first beer he'd had in a long spell, when he noticed a copy of the local paper at the end of the bar, unattended. He went around a half-dozen men and moved up to lean near it. The *Pick and Plow* was well laid out and carried yesterday's date.

A headline on an article on the back page caught his eye: *New Doing's,* and, sure enough, the first line read, *Mrs. Sarah McLaughton, who lost her husband on her way west, and her son, Tommy, have taken up residence at Hay House until she finds work or a business opportunity here. Let's all welcome her.*

Quint downed his beer and returned to the roan.

The Hay House, two blocks west, was a two-story wooden boardinghouse with a nicely trimmed yard and a covered front porch with two nice benches with goose-down pillows. But, this time of night, it was dark. However, the front door was not locked. A small podium was just inside the door, with a register open and a pen and inkwell at hand.

It was just light enough that he could read the name, *Mrs. Sarah McLaughton,* registered in dual room 8.

He moved quietly up the carpeted stairs to the second floor and had to strike a Lucifer to read the room numbers but soon found one marked 8. A soft light peeked from under the door, so she might still be awake.

He knocked lightly.

Stirring inside.

The door didn't open, but a voice, equally soft, asked, "Yes. Who's there?"

"It's Quint, ma'am."

The door opened quickly, and, to his surprise, she almost leaped upon him, hugging him tightly, and her in nothing more than a nightgown.

Then she dragged him inside.

"Where's Tommy?" he asked.

"He's in the room next door."

Then she cupped his cheeks in her hands, lifted herself on her tiptoes, and kissed him on the mouth. A chaste kiss that quickly became more.

He pushed away. "I'm embarrassed. I haven't seen bath water in more'n a week."

"You'd be welcome here had it been a year . . . but there's a tank and a tub on the back porch if you can stand cold water, and I'm sure no one's using it at this time. Don't bother shaving; I like it just the way you are."

"Then I'll excuse myself," he said, then added, "I'm so glad you're safe."

"It wasn't me in harm's way," she said. "I've hardly slept since you rode away."

"I'll be taking a bath, then riding out. I'm sure the law hereabouts won't welcome me except to a room with iron bars."

"You can ride out before light. The door will be unlocked, and I want you back here . . . to share my bed."

He eyed her for a long moment, then asked, "You sure?"

"I've never been more sure about anything, Quint. Neither my husband, nor your wife, would want us to live a lonely life."

"Then I'll be back . . . but I'll have to move on."

She smiled. "I think Spokane or even Seattle would be a good place."

He smiled to match hers. "Good as any," he said and chuckled as he headed for the back stairs.

AUTHOR'S NOTE

I hope you've enjoyed these short stories, some purely fiction but many closely based on actual history and the characters who made our West, and Manifest Destiny, so crucial to the creation of a United States from the Atlantic to the Pacific. *Eye for Eye* is soon to be a major motion picture, probably available for viewing by the time you read this. I hope you'll watch for, and enjoy, this exciting tale.

ABOUT THE AUTHOR

L. J. Martin is the author of over sixty-eight Westerns, mysteries, and thrillers. He lives in Montana with his wife, *New York Times* bestselling romantic suspense author Kat Martin. The Martins winter in Prescott, Arizona. See www.ljmartin.com for more info.

The employees of Five Star Publishing hope you have enjoyed this book.

Our Five Star novels explore little-known chapters from America's history, stories told from unique perspectives that will entertain a broad range of readers.

Other Five Star books are available at your local library, bookstore, all major book distributors, and directly from Five Star/Gale.

Connect with Five Star Publishing

Website:
gale.com/five-star

Facebook:
facebook.com/FiveStarCengage

Twitter:
twitter.com/FiveStarCengage

Email:
FiveStar@cengage.com

For information about titles and placing orders:
(800) 223-1244
gale.orders@cengage.com

To share your comments, write to us:
Five Star Publishing
Attn: Publisher
10 Water St., Suite 310
Waterville, ME 04901